Fulgentius

ALSO BY CÉSAR AIRA FROM NEW DIRECTIONS

Artforum

Birthday

Conversations

Dinner

The Divorce

Ema, the Captive

An Episode in the Life of a Landscape Painter

Ghosts

The Hare

How I Became a Nun

The Linden Tree

The Literary Conference

The Little Buddhist Monk and The Proof

The Miracle Cures of Dr. Aira

The Musical Brain

The Seamstress and the Wind

Shantytown

Varamo

Fulgentius

•

CÉSAR AIRA

translated by Chris Andrews

A NEW DIRECTIONS PAPERBOOK ORIGINAL

Originally published by Penguin Random House Grupo Editorial, S. A. U., Barcelona, in 2020; published in conjunction with the Literary Agency Michael Gaeb / Berlin

Manufactured in the United States of America
First published as a New Directions Paperbook (NDP1555) in 2023
Design by Erik Rieselbach

Library of Congress Cataloging-in-Publication Data
Names: Aira, César, 1949– author. | Andrews, Chris, 1962– translator.
Title: Fulgentius / César Aira ; translated by Chris Andrews.
Other titles: Fulgentius. English
Description: New York : New Directions Publishing Corporation, 2023.
Identifiers: LCCN 2022037755 | ISBN 9780811231695 (paperback) |
ISBN 9780811231701 (ebook)
Subjects: LCSH: Pannonia—History—Fiction. |
Rome—History—Severans, 193-235—Fiction. | LCGFT: Novels.
Classification: LCC PQ7798.1.I7 F8513 2023 | DDC 863/.64—dc23/eng/20220817
LC record available at https://lccn.loc.gov/2022037755

10 9 8 7 6 5 4 3 2 1

New Directions Books are published for James Laughlin
by New Directions Publishing Corporation
80 Eighth Avenue, New York 10011

FULGENTIUS

Quae fama modo venit ad aures?

Iungentur ante saeva sideribus freta
Et ignis undae, Tartaro tristi polus
Lux alma tenebris, roscidae nocti dies
Quam cum scelesti ...

ALL THROUGH THE SLOW RECITATIVE, THE VOICES OF
the chorus rang out in unison, filling the air of the amphitheater as if with the dark spirals of destiny conjured by the lines.
This test of the spectator's patience underlined mortality's terrible delays. The Legate Fulgentius had insisted that the actors deliver the lines as slowly as they could without allowing
the words to fall apart. He felt they were doing a good job but
couldn't tell how objective or biased his judgment might be.
He didn't know whether his status as author should make him
more or less demanding. Either he should have been pleased
with everything because it was his play, or with nothing because
the performance was bound to betray the work's ideal content.
He was finding it difficult to adopt the correct attitude to his
own creation, if the distinction between correct and incorrect
was valid in the realm of art. He wasn't a professional dramatist;
he had written a single tragedy, and it had completely exhausted
his fund of inspiration. So his assessment was based on the satisfaction of an author's minimal requirements: that the actors
articulate clearly and not skip any lines. He was reciting along
with them silently, absorbed in the action and the emotions.

3

The actor playing Fulgentius was younger than the author, which underscored the pathos of the heartrending finale. His physique was not ideal; Fulgentius would have preferred someone taller, and had in fact hesitated between the actor who finally got the part and another whose stature was imposing. He would have liked to see himself represented by a fine figure of a man, but the voice and gestures of the taller actor were so inadequate, and the other one, though short and rustic-looking, was so much better in those respects that there was really no comparison. Fulgentius was counting on the text, with its poetic force and emotive reach, to create an illusion strong enough to eclipse the actor's unfortunate appearance. Also, in that steeply raked amphitheater in Vindobona, the audience would be looking down at the actors, which would make their relative heights less noticeable.

Fulgentius generally abstained from intervening in the distribution of roles or in any aspect of production. He felt he owed that much, at least, to the actors who had agreed to interrupt their program in order to stage his tragedy, usually with just a few days in which to study the text and rehearse. But when it came to the protagonist—that is, Fulgentius himself, in all his raw humanity, complete with name and rank—he made an exception. The choice affected him too intimately to be left to chance. This was the one precaution he had to take; nothing mortified him more than the thought of the audience laughing. He had striven for sublimity, and the sublime is only a step away from the ridiculous. But his one precaution was suf-

ficient because all the dramatic action revolved around the protagonist, and as long as he played his part well the rest would be
excusable, however bad it was.

Drama worked its spell on him once more, as it always did,
and he could not imagine it failing to produce the same effect
on the other spectators. The story prevailed over all other stories, occupied every last corner of mental space: a kind of forgetting brought about by memory's most exact reconstruction.
The actors were transformed into fictional beings; the stage
gave onto the region where the self-created Fulgentius had met
his fate; time itself underwent a mutation: an afternoon in civi-
lized Vindobona became a dreadful midnight on the steppe.
Swept away by the illusion, mutely mouthing each syllable of
each hexameter, Fulgentius was so absorbed that he seemed to
be in a trance. But the trance was not too deep to prevent him
from surreptitiously observing the reactions of the audience.
So far the provincial dignitaries sitting around him, senior officials and their wives, had listened in respectful silence; they
seemed to be paying attention, although sometimes attentive-
ness was hard to distinguish from boredom. Accustomed as
they were to official functions and the deep tedium of ceremonies (which Fulgentius knew all too well), those bureaucrats
had long since perfected the art of allowing their minds to wan-
der without letting it show.

He was more curious about the thoughts of those who had
come of their own free will, neither invited nor obliged. They
were an enigma to him: sometimes he imagined that they

matched his own deep immersion in the work, but at other times he noticed them losing interest, resorting to irony, or succumbing to boredom. He was somewhat relieved to know, or trust, that in the provinces there were fewer of those smug, theatrical know-it-alls so common in Rome, fussy about epodes and antistrophes and other rhetorical matters of which he knew nothing. Fulgentius had personal reasons for preferring naive identification, unconcerned with technicalities, the response of the common man, subject as he was himself to the ups and downs of life under the empire. Although he had entered the world of theater via the back door, he resembled the professionals in regarding the audience as a mystery; and yet that impenetrable human jungle, precisely because it was impenetrable, might provide a niche for someone capable of perfect understanding.

Fulgentius did not require his legionaries or officers to attend; he didn't even suggest it. A few did come, more for lack of other things to do than out of interest. Of the six thousand men he had brought with him, enough to fill the largest amphitheater, he saw a few dozen socializing on the tiers. The rest of the audience were locals. Unlike them, his soldiers had an excuse: they had "already seen it." As if repetition were not the essence of theater and its main attraction. But how could he get that across to the coarse legionaries chewing on their rock-hard bread? He knew something about repetition: as well as having written the tragedy, he had attended each and every performance of it.

Without losing track of the play, he glanced discreetly at the higher tiers and saw that they were sparsely occupied. It was a cold day; that had to be taken into account. Even so ... Why did they make amphitheaters so big? He was aware that they were used for purposes other than theater, such as the Panathenaea and other large-scale events. But they were fundamentally ill-suited to tragedy, despite the warrant of a thousand-year tradition. Apart from the fact that the actors had to strain their voices if they weren't using megaphones, precious details of expression were lost, and distance hindered identification, the cornerstone of the tragedian's art. He would have pleaded for closet drama had he felt that the time was ripe for such an innovation. To be honest, Fulgentius himself was not ripe: he was a product of the Roman Empire, with all the limitations imposed upon him by the stage of civilization into which he had been born.

Meanwhile, the play was about halfway through. The Legate's mind had wandered for a few seconds but his lips had automatically continued their mute recitation of the lines that were being delivered on stage. And now, once more, he gave the play his full and fervent attention. The time had come for the episodes that he always found the most moving, which led by twisted but inexorable paths to the fatal dénouement.

From that point on all that mattered to him was what happened to the characters; and one of them, his alter ego, drew him into a game of conflicting perspectives. The Fulgentius on stage was negotiating in good faith with the Scythian commander, who was promising a sham alliance, while the Fulgentius seated in the audience knew that the character was being led into a trap but could do nothing to warn him, or warn himself ... This impossibility arose because there was yet another Fulgentius, the one who had written the tragedy in accordance with the strict rules of the art.

As the play came to an end, with the chorus intoning its long recitative from the back of a stage that was empty but for the body of the protagonist, slain by the Scythian king's henchmen, Fulgentius was overwhelmed by emotion. As if he had slipped into another temporal dimension, he mouthed the lines silently but with a delay of one line at first, then two, then three ... His gaze remained fixed on the corpse of the man who in the previous acts had been a valiant warrior, the pride of the imperial legions, and now lay there lifeless, his lost soul wandering in the dim underworld. Pity gripped the general's chest, returning him to the real world. The same thing happened every time: it was no use telling himself that it wasn't true, that he was still alive and would live on for years to come. Seeing himself die in a poetic fiction was still a kind of death.

His gloominess had a correlative and a partial cause in reality: the sun had set and night was deepening. The spectators got up; Fulgentius did his best to compose himself and rid his face of the tensions engendered by the play. He turned to Lucius Cordatus, the governor of the province, who congratulated him:

"An admirable portrait of a hero."

To which the governor's wife added: "I've never been so moved by a death."

What would they know? Their praise, although well mean-ing and even sincere, glanced off the surface of the work, get-ting no purchase on the substance in which its value lay. As Fulgentius listened to them, he felt that his tragedy was taking off into the sky; each adjective they used to describe it was a spring that boosted its flight. It was pure courtesy, empty words dictated by etiquette. Perhaps it was better that way, after all. He looked around for his assistant, Lactarius, called him over and gave him some strict and bluntly worded orders. They were un-necessary, but it was a way to recover his sense of reality, like a pearl diver coming up for air. (The pearl he had brought back from his plunge was his own imagined and represented death.)

Accompanied by a selection of dignitaries, Fulgentius made his way to the pit to speak with the actors. Seeing the man who had played his part alive and well, with rosy sausage-eater's cheeks, came as a relief tinged with disappointment, as if the compassion spent on him had been wasted. But the Legate con-gratulated the actor and the rest of the cast without having to lie or exaggerate.

Nor did he have to lie later on, at the farewell dinner put on by Governor Cordatus, when asked if he was happy with the production. He pronounced it excellent.

"So the city's honor is safe," said one of the guests. "Your opinion is decisive, since an author must be the most demand-ing of spectators."

"Not necessarily," Fulgentius replied. "Of course, there are authors and authors, and there must be some who are never satisfied. But I'm not like that, perhaps because I'm not a professional. I'm open to diverse interpretations and welcome the differences, as long as the text itself is respected."

"What did you think of our city?"

"Magnificent. Superb."

"Is this your first visit to Vindobona?"

He had noticed this before: whenever literature came up, people were generally inclined or even eager to change the subject. They continued to do so, in this case, until the governor called for a toast to the distinguished visitor who was about to leave them. In his reply the Legate thanked his hosts for the many kindnesses they had shown him, mentioning in particular how much he had enjoyed the "excellent" performance of his faltering, amateur venture into the dramatic arts. False modesty aside, his praise was sincere, and partly motivated by what lay ahead. He was sure that there would not be another production worth seeing and hearing for a long time, in all the months and years of his mission in barbarian lands.

After a while, the replenishment of the wine bowls led to franker and louder effusions. Gratuitous outbursts of laughter alternated with quarrels about gladiators and quadrigae. The marble of the august Roman tongue degenerated into watery clay. The lamps gave off red smoke; heads bobbed.

"What must he be thinking of us?"

So wondered a matron who seemed to be very comfortably settled on the couch of a triclinium, her troubling gaze veiled by half-closed or half-open eyelids, her breasts emerging from the disordered folds of her gown.

"*Ut vobis*, Madam."

It came out spontaneously, as if someone else had spoken through him.

Peals of laughter entwined themselves around him like so many cobras. Suddenly he felt that he was at the center of a vortex of drunks. An abstemious man, he had stuck to water. He felt, as he often did when people were drinking around him, that he was in the midst of a multitude, as if the wine-induced repetition were affecting him and not the others.

He took leave of the banquet and went off to bed with a perfect excuse: the legion would be departing at dawn. The farewells were perfunctory, given the state of the hosts, who slurred the few words they could muster. The faithful Lactarius was waiting in the portico, where the icy air revived the Legate. Forgoing his lodgings in the palace, where he had slept since arriving in the city, he went to his tent, where reveille would find him ready to set forth.

It was time to be gone, high time. What had been planned as a two-day stop for taking on supplies had stretched to three long weeks. He should have felt guilty about the delay and abusing the hospitality extended to him by the good Cordatus, who had no real choice in the matter. But the legion was grateful for the rest, and he had treated himself to a production of his play. That had been his reason for lingering in Vindobona: to give the local theater troupe time to learn the roles and rehearse. That city was the last outpost of culture on his route, and he didn't want to miss the chance of laying down a comforting memory that would stay with him through all the trials of the campaign. He realized that this was a personal reason, to say the least, for halting a mass of six thousand men and draining the region's resources almost to the point of exhaustion. But it was his prerogative; once out of the senate's reach, he answered to no one and nothing other than his own sovereign whims. Besides, it was wrong to speak of a delay: Rome was eternal, and the empire encompassed the world, transcending petty domestic calculations of time and space.

AT SIXTY-SEVEN, FABIUS EXELSUS FULGENTIUS WAS one of Rome's most illustrious and experienced generals. With his record of long and distinguished service, he was an indispensable element in any expansionist plans requiring the participation of the armed forces, as they all did, inevitably. He had commanded legions in hundreds of campaigns, from one end of the empire to the other, boldly or warily, thinking ahead, a scholar of strategy, exploiting truces, as patient as a lifeless stone when laying siege, as swift in a surprise attack as red lava rushing down the slopes of a volcano.

He might have been no more than a formidable military machine, notching up one victory after another, if not for his skills in politics and administration, where a range of problems always arose as soon as the fighting ceased. There too he had exercised rare aptitudes. Like the chimera, the Legate could be at once firm and flexible, obliging those who received his orders to wonder how they were meant to be applied. The time this wondering took allowed him to keep a step ahead. And at any point he could revert to his role as champion of the sword, striking terror into the hearts of the junior functionaries.

This veteran soldier's red sandal had sunk into the burning Libyan sands, a sable hood had protected his balding scalp on the tundra of Hibernia, the stamping of the Iberians echoed in his ears, and he could still see in his mind's eye the whirling of the dervishes. Few men of his generation had seen so much of the world; or perhaps many had, but few or none who had also conveyed the bronze eagle, the power, and the language of Rome.

Although his age and his weariness, after so many years of trying service, made him better suited to staying at home and taking his grandchildren for walks around the Forum, his name remained at the head of the list of irreplaceable generals, at least as he imagined it. He was pleased to have this confirmed when the senate sounded him out about resuming command of the legendary Lupine Legion. His family and close friends protested. They had arguments to spare, both explicit and implicit. Among the latter was the suspicion that the senators and perhaps even the imperial household were trying to get him out of the way, foreseeing a troubled succession. The most powerful explicit argument was based on the multitude of difficulties and dangers awaiting him should he accept. The attempt at dissuasion was supported by indisputable truths, but that was precisely why it clashed with the general's deep-rooted military pride.

The mission was delicate: to pacify Pannonia. The calls for help coming from that wild province, infested with Illyrian guerilla groups, had begun to concern the central authorities, who were alarmed by the prospect of chaos and collapse. Despondency and desertion were taking their toll on the troops

garrisoned in the cities; the statutes were being willfully mis-
interpreted, and the numerous exiles for whom the empire had
chosen Pannonia as a natural place of banishment were exploiting the disorder to get together and plot. The vast proportions
of the province, coupled with its aberrant topography, fostered
all manner of insurrections, which flourished as the bloodleaf
thrives in rocky hollows and river bends. The radical solution
was to go storming in with the eagles at the head of a major legion. It was a remedy that had never failed; nobody could argue
with such a long history of success.

But people asked: Wasn't the mission impossible? A legion,
especially the magnificent and undefeated Legion of the Wolf,
could be highly dissuasive for those who saw it marching behind the standards and were dazzled by the coruscating mass
of pikes and helmets. But out in the woods and the forests, with
only goats and magpies looking on, the effect was less reliable.
Wandering tribes armed to the teeth, inhabitants of volcanic
craters who lived in hamlets of black shale, horsemen with
unheard-of skills: a whole conglomeration of different and le-
thally elusive enemies, appearing and disappearing, would be
immune to intimidation. Not to mention the stinking swamps,
the rocky slopes, the thirst, the distances. The general's friends
and family stopped at nothing to talk him out of going. Per-
fidiously they asked if he had laid in sufficient supplies of the
herb for the infusion that he used to manage his urinary "is-
sues" (*minima mingendi difficultas*).

He counterattacked with a performance of resignation: Yes,

they were right, and he would have preferred to stay at home, of course he would have, but he had no choice: he was and always had been a soldier, obeying orders was what he did and must do, regardless of his natural inclination to remain in the company of his beloved family. And if it was pointed out to him that he had not, in fact, received any orders, he responded with a silence full of innuendo. He prepared his departure with a long face, sighs, and mumbled complaints ("having to march again, at my age"). In fact, he was delighted. Two long years of idleness had sorely tested his tolerance of civilian life. The days in Rome were all so alike, with the routine of the Forum and the baths, that they blurred into one another. Always the same faces, the same statue around the corner, the same columns repeated over and over, as if to taunt those who had pinned their hopes in life on variety and surprise. And there was not even the option of taking it easy and enjoying the peace and quiet, because the palace intrigues spilled out into the streets, and their virulence affected everyone. People were permanently on edge; no one was safe from straying—or being dragged—into trouble.

The life of a soldier was calmer, paradoxically. Real danger, the concrete and visible presence of an opponent bent on killing you, simplified the game; you knew where you stood. You didn't have to rack your brains trying to tell friends from enemies at boring banquets or in humiliating antechambers. The relentless nervous tension of life at the center of imperial power was such that men went to war for relief. It was also a way of getting to know different lands and peoples. The body shook off the lethargy of city life, as did the mind. Legs proved useful for something more than being crossed and uncrossed while listening to dull speeches, and the mind, confronted with urgent life-and-death questions, rid itself of frivolous litter. To what did Fulgentius owe his good physical and mental health, if not to the rigors of military toil?

There was another reason, and this too he kept to himself, although it was very close to his heart, so close it counted for as much as all the others put together: his tragedy, the work he had written so many years before, and which for some years now had accompanied him on each new campaign. His military excursions had offered ideal opportunities to have the play performed at a range of venues, since its entry into the official theater repertoire had been barred by the self-declared arbiters of taste and the envy and spite of the literary cliques. It had not even occurred to him to protest. His decision not to defend his work before the professional coryphaei was motivated partly by pride and contempt but also, fundamentally, by fear. To engage in arguments about rhetoric would have put him in a delicate position. Although he was reasonably cultivated, from a very young age his military duties had left him little time for study. He was quite prepared to agree with the pedants: perhaps his tragedy had no merit. Or not for them, but for him it did, and that was all that mattered.

The story of the tragedy was almost as old as Fulgentius himself, since it went all the way back to his childhood. Like every well-born Roman boy, he had received an excellent edu-

cation in the humanities. His preceptor was a strict traditional-
ist, who had no time for the pedagogical theories imported by
the Alexandrians. For him the only things that counted were
rhetoric (with its tried and tested rules), memorization, and
purity of language. It wasn't all suffering for the boy, who came
to enjoy the epics, once he had mastered their complex pros-
ody (the prose of the classical historians was worse). Reading
about heroic deeds of old, whether they belonged to an unverifiable reality or to the gaudy realm of myth, confirmed his military vocation, which coincided with the path chosen for him by
his family. The suffering came with the indigestible tragedies
that he was obliged to read and learn by heart. Their dreariness
made him wonder how serious people, many of whom had held
high public office, could care so little for the honor of a Roman
gentlemen as to put their names to those pathetic confections.

This vehement dismissal gave way to mockery, which in turn
triggered a particular form of action: secretly, in the time left
after lessons and riding, Fulgentius began to write a tragedy of
his own. The aim was to show how silly the genre was, applying
the rules with ludicrous rigidity, turning the mortal seriousness
of the tragic into one more joke.

The most interesting transformation was the one that con-
verted the boredom of reading into the euphoria of writing. He
let the meter guide him; it gathered in all sorts of unexpected
words. Once he realized that the meaning was developing on
its own, he gave it little thought. The general idea was to trace
a heroic destiny, with all the standard clichés exaggerated for

comic effect. The protagonist was a general whose chronic incompetence led to his demise at the hands of shadowy foreigners. Fulgentius gave the character his own name, as a kind of signature. He enjoyed the task so much he could have continued indefinitely, had he not been so eager to show the results to his preceptor.

He made a fair copy and presented it as a lost tragedy by Livius Andronicus, recently discovered in a Sicilian library. The fraud could not be sustained beyond the second guffaw. The preceptor went on reading it aloud, right to the end, choking with laughter, to which the boy responded in kind. The master congratulated his pupil. It was no small feat for a lad of twelve to have produced such an accomplished pastiche; it showed that he had grasped the workings of the most prestigious dramatic genre, if only to subject them to humorous subversion. The work's lack of seriousness was due to its purely literary nature: the product of a mind intoxicated by reading (here the preceptor had to plead guilty), it owed nothing to experience, which the boy did not yet have. It was undeniably impertinent, but the hexameters scanned well, and since the joke would be confined to the family circle, there was no harm done.

As it turned out, the confinement was less than perfect. The preceptor mentioned the charming prank to his pupil's parents, who read the play. Certain uncles, hearing about it, expressed their curiosity and borrowed the scrolls. Meanwhile the young author, whose life was rich in distractions, diversions and discoveries, forgot all about his tragedy, for three decades at least.

During one of the Panathenaic festivals, when Fulgentius, a renowned general by this stage, happened to be in Rome between campaigns, an acquaintance asked him if he knew about a tragedy that shared his name. This man had been struck by the coincidence, since the name was not very common. Fulgentius said he knew nothing about it and showed no interest. That would have been the end of it if his interlocutor had not carried on regardless, explaining that he had attended a performance the previous night, at one of the orgiastic events, and had been struck by the crazy strangeness of the work: formally, it was a tragedy according to the rules of the genre but the content was completely wild ... He was struggling to explain, it was so unlike anything he had ever seen, so he resorted to examples. One of them, involving a Scythian king, rang a faint bell for Fulgentius, and the sound went rippling through his mind in concentric waves.

Tantalized, that very night he went to the Panathenaic complex where the festival was being celebrated, and not without effort, pushing through a mob of malodorous drunks, reached the place where the work in question was being performed. It was indeed his tragedy. How had it come to be staged there? He never knew for sure. He supposed that the scrolls had been left in a relative's library, which had been dispersed when its owner died; and given all the twists and turns of manuscript transmission, it was not implausible that they had fallen into the hands of a theater company.

The play was a colossal shock to Fulgentius. His ears and memory took the lines in simultaneously; he repossessed them like lost and precious property. He had come to be the general he had imagined as a boy, by divine intervention, it seemed. This realization of dreams involved a shift from joking to seriousness, for him at least, although the rest of the audience was cracking up. He was overcome by emotion, and it didn't matter that the actors were clowns; he saw through their motley, heard through their squawking. He saw himself, facing the inexorable destiny conferred on him by Poetry. Everything took on meaning; everything was illuminated.

In the final climax, when the cruel hyperborean steel pierced his heart, a profusion of pain and pleasure filled his eyes with tears. Amidst the shouts and guffaws and the tumbling of the clowns, he was conquering death, claiming it as a promise of life. The impression might not have been so strong if the staging had been less derisive and coarse. As it was, it allowed him to cut himself off and elaborate his feelings without interference.

From that moment on, Fulgentius could not rest until he saw the play again. And this revived his military career, because he realized that it would be much easier to arrange performances in the provinces than in Rome. So he connived to secure the command of the next replacement legions destined for Gaul (he would never have stooped to such a maneuver for any other reason), hired scribes to make dozens of copies of the play, and treated himself to five performances, each with a different cast, in five Gallic cities. It was a rediscovery each time. The following year, it was Hispania. Then Alexandria, Anglia, Germania. And now it was time for Pannonia.

The desire to see another performance of his tragedy had been growing over the last two years spent in the capital. He had received his new mission at just the right time. He knew that Pannonia was still half wild, which meant that it would be rich in mystery, and he was sure that in the far reaches of the empire he would find human material well suited to the theater. To begin with, he had chosen a route that passed through the sophisticated city of Vindobona, where he could expect the production to be decent. So it was, and the following day Fulgentius set off at the head of his columns, returning in thought to what he had witnessed the previous afternoon, which was easy to reconstruct since he knew the text by heart.

DAY WAS BREAKING. A GOLDEN LIGHT WAS SPREADING in the east. Then it all turned crystal clear, and little lilac-colored clouds began to ride on the breezes. Next, the white and the green. In the distance, the Danubian Alps reared like formidable stone giants guarding the Pannonian plains. All the birds flew off in that direction. The mountains were like children, but nobody thought of mountains when they saw a child. The farmers with their carts full of produce were converging on the city that the legion was leaving behind. As they passed, they tossed turnips or carrots to the soldiers, who leaped to catch them, laughing. They too were like children. Silence hung over the voices. Dawn turned out to be too large even for the multitude. The broad paved road fell silent too. The mist lingered. The legionaries must have been thinking that they would never get anywhere if the world went on speaking the language of the mountains, persisting in their childish babble. Because of the mountains they had to wait, as one has to wait for children to grow up; the mountains seemed to be growing too but, as with children, only time would tell if they would be of any use when fully grown.

Fulgentius was riding a white horse with a gait as smooth as silk. His personal assistant Lactarius, a young man from a good family, followed a few steps behind, on a less noble mount. He rode up abreast of the general and asked his permission to speak. There was really no need to ask, since his conversation was an asset on long marches. That was why Fulgentius had promoted him to his personal staff, despite his tender age—still a boy really, ten years before, at the time of his recruitment—though later, the general felt vindicated when he saw how efficient the young man was, rendering half of the staff redundant. His capacities were clearly innate.

"I am curious to know, your Excellency, why we are entering Pannonia via Vindobona, which seems to be more of an exit, to judge from the map."

There was no point replying that the same door can serve as entrance and exit. Doors that served one of those purposes to the exclusion of the other had not yet been invented. In any case the question was tinged with irony and had been sufficiently answered the previous afternoon. That was how it was between them. They didn't trade questions and answers for the conventional purpose of sharing information but as a way of passing the time, indulging in playful backchat.

"I must admit I was a little confused there for a while, with Dalmatia and Dacia and so on. Maps are conventional, after all, as well as incomplete. But white Vindobona, with its palaces and mirages, was an acceptable starting point. And I don't think there's any reason to regret my choice—"

"None at all."

"... especially after yesterday."

"It was an excellent production, your Excellency."

"First rate."

"Unforgettable."

The general didn't go on because there was a whiff of mockery in the air. You could never tell with Lactarius.

"Although I've seen it so many times, I'm always discovering something new. This time I noticed an expression that, if I may say so, puzzled me. 'The Mothers violated my Thought.' What does that mean?"

Fulgentius furrowed his brow, trying to remember which character said those words, and in which scene. He soon gave up. Although he knew the whole tragedy by heart, he knew it line by line, from the beginning to the end, and he couldn't plunge into the middle to find something; he would have had to start from the first line and keep going until he came to that one.

"It's such a long time since I wrote it."

He thought it opportune to change the subject:

"Everything in order with the legion?"

He turned to look back. The column of marching men, broken up by carts and companies of horsemen, wound away into the distance and out of sight among the wooded hills. The standard bearers were still wearing the wolfskin caps that symbolized the legion, but they would take them off when the sun began to beat down and there were no more spectators. This vestige of totemism was far below the intellectual level of an educated Roman like Fulgentius. But he was not averse to a touch of harmless primitivism as an antidote, although purely symbolic, to the decadent refinement that came with civilization. Refinement persisted, nevertheless, in the coordination required to transform those thousands of souls into one great war machine. It had taken centuries to oil that machine to the point where there was nothing lacking or in excess. Its functioning required ceaseless vigilance and superhuman attention. Everything had to be in place at just the right moment: food, lodgings, wages, medical supplies, chains of command, arms, schedules, scouting parties, and a hundred other things. The logistics were infernal, and after long and futile efforts, Fulgentius had given up trying to understand them. They worked, and that was all that mattered. If keeping his attention as taut as a bowstring was what he was meant to be doing, too bad. He considered himself an impractical dreamer, better suited to contemplating a landscape than to laying out a camp's geometrical grid. When called upon to resolve a problem, he turned to Lactarius, for whom that immense hieroglyph held no secrets. How the young man knew what to do was beyond Fulgentius. He gave the impression that he had been born with the knowledge. Perhaps it was one of the privileges of the young. If so, youth was to be drawn out for as long as possible.

Both in reality and in the general's dreams, the legion that had fallen to his charge—those six thousand men with their glorious history and bulky equipment—seemed a dark bubble full of mystery, obeying his orders as blindly as the stars obey the laws of the cosmos.

The legion was a city in movement. Fulgentius had sensed this as soon as he began to live in one and rose (via the usual *cursus honorum*) to be its commander. The number of inhabitants was not the only ground of resemblance. Within the legion there were also streets and passages, bridges, towers, and basements, not all of them metaphorical. Like a city, the legion could never be completely known; there were always suburbs or corners where one had never set foot. What treasures of intelligence or tenderness might its ranks conceal, wondered the man at its head. What poisonous traps of fraud or crime? What stores of courage? Or of cowardice? Like a multicolored carpet spread over the earth, studded with furry pompoms (the soldiers' matted manes), the vast contingent kept slowly advancing.

Yes, yes, thought Fulgentius, his mission consisted of going to Pannonia, wherever that was, and imposing order by force. But the functions of the legion would always be subordinate to its reality, and reality was what came to be without an ulterior aim.

The green valleys gave out a week later, along with the hills and knolls; it was time to tackle the mountains. It had made sense, on the plains, to think of the legion as a city, but the analogy was better forgotten once they reached the indomitable Alps, because having to transport a city through the mountains, even metaphorically, was dispiriting. It was uphill all the way, for a start: advancing to new levels of coldness, gritting one's teeth against the sheer climb. There was no point delegating tasks. The centurions became decurions. The humble crevice-dwelling spiders had the privilege of remaining where they were; the lichens didn't even have to spin. The columns negotiated mountain passes, peered down into chasms, were struck blind by the glare off the snow, or advanced in single file along a narrow cornice, taking all day, from dawn until midnight, to cross that precarious natural bridge. The scouts from the advance parties came back with bad news. To be faced with flooding in the uplands seemed the acme of misfortune.

"I have already started dreaming of mountains," said Fulgentius one night, as the slave boy rubbed balm into his feet.

During the crossing, and no doubt under the influence of the visions populating his dreams, he began to worry about the descent. The fear was not unfounded, given his image-based reasoning. The effort of climbing had held the legion together, but once it left the high peaks behind and began to rush downhill, it would spill forward in a headlong jumble, and there would be no way to restore its original form. Fulgentius shared his worries with some of the centurions, who reassured him. He was letting his thought be swayed by the unconscious memory of a common experience: accidentally breaking a vase. The legion, as opposed to a vase, had the flexibility of the human, which meant that it would return to its original form automatically.

"True," he admitted. "If the mind serves any purpose, it is to create attractions."

They felt like gods up there, among the eternal snows. As if they were setting foot on a permanent reality. The scarcity of oxygen dissipated their worries. And suddenly, when they had

begun to think it would never happen, they had arrived. There
they were on the platforms that had been awaiting them. They
spent a few days regrouping. Hunting parties set out, and the
men explored the surroundings, getting used to the idea that
they had reached Pannonia.

But had they really? After all, "Pannonia" was only a name,
and the place where they were was just another place: the sun
that shone down on them was the same, and it was a safe bet
that the moon, when it came out, would be the same too. They
were breathing the air they had always breathed. And yet everything was different, marvelously different. If that was an illusion, they accepted it joyfully. But when they remembered that
the illusion was a product of the empire that they represented,
they grew serious: it was time to leave preconceptions behind
and take up the campaign in the present. As always, the Legate
turned to his assistant. The maps? Lactarius had memorized
them all.

On this occasion memory had played him false, according to
the men. The art of memory had a deep tendency to lapse into
brute accumulation. And when that happened, mental maps
appeared in reverse, like figures reflected in a mirror. The mirror was faithful but left and right changed places in the image,
and that could be hazardous when planning a battle.

"The flight of the birds, the march of the ants, the roar of
the wind, and the whispering of dreams will show us the way."

"BRING THE INTERPRETER!" THE GENERAL SHOUTED angrily, ten times a day.

It was always the same: he had to send for someone who knew the language of the prisoner or the peasant, then he had to wait patiently and trust that the man they brought actually knew the language in question and had enough wit to understand what was required of him. It was never the same interpreter, which infuriated Fulgentius. If he gave the order to keep an interpreter on hand at all times, it created no end of confusion: anyone could be an interpreter, or not. The men of the legion spoke twenty or thirty different languages; many thought they could understand the Illyrian dialects and launched into guttural orations with an irresponsible confidence. They grew bolder still interrogating prisoners to extract intelligence. But in the chaos of advances and retreats, which jumbled the places and times, the information was doubly confused by talking at cross purposes. The imperial project required study and planning, which did not sit well with the urgencies of war, and yet without wars there could be no empire.

It was not long before hostilities arose. A mob of horsemen came rushing out of the first village they burned, as if engendered by the flames, and the Romans had to raise their shields against the hail of arrows, form defensive circles, and mount a night watch. The rugged terrain unnerved them; they had to resort to on-the-spot interrogations, and to intepreters, with their providential linguistic skills and their exasperating impermanence.

Fulgentius lost his patience and ordered the legion to take no prisoners. It was safe to assume, he said, that they would not have to face any armies on their march, just a few opportunistic rebels. There was no point deploying the troops against them; it was enough to remain in formation, like an armored wall, until they reached the regional capitals. If the guerrilla groups were terrorizing the local population, the solution was to deprive them of victims by burning the villages. They'd never have expected such an innovative and radical response. And it would have the beneficial side effect of making interpreters redundant; Fulgentius thought of ordering his men to bring a few and crucify them, but he didn't want to waste time.

Like the weight of a giant bearing down through ankles and feet of iron, discriminating only between those who did and did not speak the marmoreal language of Latium, the legion traversed the outer ring of the province, crushing all that stood in its way. Massacre followed massacre, like punishments before the crime. Attempts at resistance were uprooted like noxious weeds, but crops and flowers fared no better. The giant's heavy tread was equivalent to the delicate brushing of a butterfly's wing: the damage they did was the same. If a forest got in the way, with its hiding places and legends, a thousand men with axes, or two or three thousand, depending on the number of trees, would cut it down, pile the trunks into a pyramid fifty cubits high, and set them alight. Juniper wood smoke shrouded the hills like a mist: an incense for which the priestesses of Ephesus would have paid with gold or their bodies. Where the legionaries found towns they left ruins; where they found ruins they marched on, with the nagging suspicion that they had passed that way before. But the suspicion was quelled by an explanation that the Legate drafted hastily and had his centurions read aloud: wandering in circles might occur in a wood but the woods had been razed, as they well knew.

There were also ruins of ancient, pre-Roman civilizations, which left a melancholy impression of death, different from the vivid, bloody death that was the soldiers' daily bread: a sense of time unfolding majestically, not contracted to the instant of a reaction. The soldiers took pottery or statues of animal gods, a stone toad or a whistle (which later they'd carelessly leave behind along the way).

Apart from the skirmishes, there were real but minor battles. The guerrilla bands that had been forced to retreat gathered to launch surprise attacks. These were by no means a serious threat, but they provided an excuse (not that one was needed) to massacre the peasants who had provided the rebels with supplies.

The arrows rained down thick and fast from every high place along the legion's route. The shields went up, forming a continuous roof, and then came the reaction. The archers were doggedly hunted down and forced to eat their arrows. The very few who escaped went into exile, and had to suffer the symbolic death of losing their land. Real rains turned the roads into sludge. The marshes grew like living creatures. Irritation and fatigue made the soldiers hurry on and fall more violently upon whatever got in their way. The butchered bodies glistened pinkly in the rain, like mud slicks reflecting a reddening sky. By the time the legionaries were halfway to the first local capital, they had made the purpose of their presence clear. No one had invited them into the rings of Pannonia, which was why they struck at them like the lash of a furious Jupiter.

The cruelty that Fulgentius witnessed from the height of his black horse was typical of the period. Acts that seem wicked now were deemed fitting, required by the realism of the age. Why were the Romans so destructive? Because they were living in the centuries of construction. Nature and civilization were born together in the unknown, and the world was there to be sacked. Indeed, the empire should have destroyed more. It was stopping short. According to ancient wisdom, which the new people had taken up, an active evil was better than a passive good. Good resided in thought, evil in action. Men had to give their worst instincts free rein, and prey on each other like wild animals. Evil and good were subordinate to the active and the passive. It wasn't impossible that one day the poles might change places and good take the lead. The doing of evil might even be prohibited; people might come to disapprove of killing for the hell of it or raping for fun or burning down a house with seven children inside. It wasn't impossible but the prospect was dispiriting. In fact, the seed of that reversal was already latent in the current situation.

Fulgentius didn't have much faith in the dominant philosophy or in any other. He found them all too general. He was more at home in the particular, where all philosophies were of equal value. That was why he let events take their course and contemplated their unfolding from an Olympian distance. The world around him was too busy with its own processes to pay attention to him or anyone else. People could do what they liked without being brought to account. Gazing at one of the little flowers peeping out of the mud, he thought: "If it's true that some flowers are hermaphrodites, I'm allowed to do anything."

He also gazed at the human remains left after the battle. He had grown accustomed to death, but still he went on noticing it. He saw a very young man lying dead, his long black hair spread out on the grass like a wing. The body was intact. This transcended the accidental. He ordered Lactarius to close the man's eyes.

"He looks as if he's sleeping."

"Could it have been a heart attack?"

"Quite possibly," said the Legate, viewing the grim scene from a height, still astride his enormous horse. "The heart betrays the young and the strong, turning all its strength against them. This young man may well have suffered from a congenital weakness of the small valves surrounding the heart; the

slightness of his limbs suggests as much. His physical consti-
tution is at odds with the stern, fierce expression on his face,
set there by his will, I suppose. Thrown into the brutal life of
a soldier, he tried to repress his gentle, peace-loving, feminine
nature, and had to live with the resulting tension. When the
first clash came, it was too much for him."

"A plausible theory, though based on little concrete evidence."

"There's nothing more concrete than a dead body. In fact,
it's only in a dead body that the concrete makes itself manifest.
People are abstract as long as they live."

But words expired before the dream of the handsome Van-
dal. The Legate's mind went wandering. "This is my work," he
thought, "my creation." Among the thousands of dead bodies
that resulted from a campaign, he chose one, just as he had
found it, to be the object of his calm contemplation. That immobility reminded him of something, but what? The feeling
transcended compassion. He was thinking of his own life, of
the discontinuity in his youth. When he finally spoke, it was to
order the men to build a cube on the site out of fine wooden
rods, with four hollow, disposable stelae on each side, and
feather plumes dyed red. That night, by the sole light of the
stars, they were to douse the structure with flammable oils and
set it ablaze. He doubted that they would carry out his orders
but found satisfaction enough in the concept. This was just the
latest in a series of fanciful, extravagant ideas (it was modest
compared to many of the others) emanating from a second Fulgentius who lay dormant within the first. As usual, the slave boy

was squatting beneath the general's horse. It was the only place on the vast fields of war and peace where he was invisible to his master: directly beneath him, in the transparent, inviolable hideaway marked out by the horse's four hooves. Fulgentius told him to get out of there immediately.

ONCE THE SOLDIERS HAD BREACHED THE RING OF CON-
flict, they passed with barely a halt through two small Rhaetian
cities, which sent delegations of quaestors with greetings and
provisions. The quaestors had learned of the legion's cleaning-
up operations and were duly grateful, which didn't stop them
making requests and complaining. Their themes were predictable: the falling price of wheat, the flooding caused by deficient
public works, and as always the promised but undelivered tax
cuts. Before they could get to the cuts, they always had to beat
around the bush. No one knew who had made the promise, and
a gentlemen's agreement forbade them to ask. The mental firmament of the empire's tributaries was constellated with myth-
ical promises, made when Rome and time itself were young.

The legion didn't tarry long in those mediocre urban out
posts, just long enough to check that everything was more or
less in order. The columns marched on, passing plowed fields,
flocks, and vineyards. Children ran to see them, and storks took
flight as they went by, unfolding like beautiful ideas about nothing in particular. The constant autumn sun accompanied them
with its customary punctuality. It was a walk in the park.

Although the region seemed to be reasonably Romanized,
Fulgentius didn't even bother to inquire about local theater and

the possibility of putting on his tragedy. He would regret this later on, when he came to see how flexible the play was, how well it responded to different stages, casts, and sets of props. He would come to lament the opportunities he had missed by adhering to his original idea of drama as something that could take place only in a big official amphitheater, with all the traditional, cumbersome pomp. Later experience revealed that the text of his tragedy was as light as air, adapting itself to the tiniest speck of dust but equally to the vastness of the sky. Not that he deserved any credit: all writing had the same elasticity, by virtue of being a thing of the mind.

Fulgentius would learn all this on the journey. For the moment his first goal was Carnuntum, an important, long-established city, where there would no doubt be acting troupes, facilities, and above all interest. Again he was jumping to conclusions. This lazy mental habit had led him to believe that an interest in the theater could only exist among audiences who had regularly attended formal productions. That was another prejudice, which crumbled when he saw for himself that theater was like dreaming: it wasn't an acquired taste; its spell could work on anyone.

He hurried on and had the centurions promise the men a long rest once they arrived. Although eventually fulfilled, the promise was unnecessary. The veteran Lupine legionaries needed no incentive to obey orders. And marching now among flowers and birds, beside a broad blue river jumping with fish whose snow-white flesh the locals supplied, they could have gone on accelerating indefinitely.

At night the legion seemed to dissolve into dark atoms. The watchmen walked up and down the sleeping rows. After an early evening meal, the Legate withdrew to his tent and checked the copies of his tragedy. He kept the numbered scrolls in order, in a chest that was his most treasured possession; if he lost it, the journey would lose all meaning. Or so he made out, but he knew it wouldn't be so bad. He had secreted a second chest in the rearguard, with the same contents as the first, telling no one, not even the faithful Lactarius. It was a personal superstition: in this matter, he was unwilling to take any risks. His reasoning was as follows: one chest, the one he kept close, was treated with all the respect befitting precious cargo; all the officers and porters knew that it contained the irreplaceable scrolls of the Legate's tragedy, with which they saw him retiring to his tent every night. But in spite of all the precautions taken, or even because of them, the contents of that chest might be lost or damaged. By contrast, the duplicate chest was riding like one more piece of gear with the least valuable and guarded items (replacement sandals, dried apples, flints). If something happened to what had been most carefully protected, the simplest reckoning of odds suggested that what had been neglected would be safe.

Although the general had already checked the order of the scrolls, as he did every day, he checked again, not driven by an obsessive compulsion but drawn by the pleasure it gave him. And there could be no harm in making sure. Long experience had taught him to plan for the contingencies awaiting him in the city ahead. He undertook the checking, which prepared the way for sleep, with the powers of the sleeping mind. Even without reading a word, merely handling the scrolls filled him with a vaguely theatrical feeling, which, in the silence and solitude of the night, intensified to rapture. When he saw the play performed, it became present and real to him: memory blended with attention, and he felt alive, relishing each instant and each line. But it was what it was and nothing more; such were the limitations of the real. Physical contact with the script, on the other hand, conjured up the infinite variations to which the play might lend itself. There was no ideal production, thankfully. Each one went on changing in time. For Fulgentius, alone in his tent (the slave boy was sleeping, Lactarius was playing dice with his friends: muffled voices, the clicking of the little bones, and the crackling of the fire could be heard in the distance), theater's unreality made everything unreal. When he woke up in the morning, he couldn't remember how the session had ended, and wondered if the scrolls had been properly put away, keeping each copy separate and the five acts in the right order. He resolved to check them again that night.

The journey continued for a couple of weeks in flat country, until they spied the towers of Carnuntum on the horizon. Fulgentius didn't know the city, but according to the information that he gathered as they drew near, it was a large, wealthy, teeming metropolis. These descriptions had to be taken with a grain of salt, coming from peasants and villagers who called a group of ten houses a city. But Carnuntum was bound to be prosperous, to judge from what they had seen on the plains: the flocks, the crops, even the unguarded hamlets, a sign of peace and stability. None of these details escaped the Legate's sharp eye. If he could dispense with military operations, there would be more time for what really interested him. All the wealth produced by the lush and fertile meadowlands to the south of the Danube flowed to Carnuntum. He wondered if the skirmishes with Rhaetians and Vandals might not have already accomplished his mission: Pannonia proper didn't seem to be in any need of pacification. In that case, the rumors circulating before his departure might have been true: perhaps the real reason for the expedition was to remove him and the formidable Lupine Legion from Rome, and prevent him from intervening in the struggles for succession. As this thought occurred to him, a smile of secret superiority spread over his face. If they had intended to harm him, they had completely missed the mark. They couldn't have done him a greater favor: what this make-believe campaign meant in practice was a delightful excursion through idyllic landscapes, healthy exercise, banquets, and new productions of his tragedy (not to mention the benefits of a spell away from home and family obligations).

He mentioned none of this to his staff. On the contrary, he spoke of toughening discipline, sharpening the spears, reinforcing the shields, tightening up the organization of the watches. No one took him seriously, but since it was for the good of all, there were no objections.

In conversation with his assistant Lactarius, he could relax and be more open. The well-established fact that the empire had enemies everywhere had always struck him, he said, as a solution rather than a problem. The most likely outcome was that they would end up killing each other. Assuming the role of enemies obliged them to take up arms and live in a state of war. And since they were powerless against the invincible Roman legions, they would have to discharge their pent-up belligerence in battles with fellow enemies.

The young man did not appear to be convinced. For the sheer pleasure of debate, or merely to pass the time, Fulgentius tried another tack.

He said that sometimes a single death sufficed. He based this assertion on a phenomenon that Pliny had observed: in a large animal population, made up of millions, all the members of a species, a single premature death could lead to a mass extinction, so tangled were the causal chains of life or the processes gathered under that name. Although there was no a priori way to identify the key individual in a group, such an individual existed, somewhere, and the survival of all the others depended on its hidden presence. That was why society took such a dim view of death, especially the death of the young.

"I don't know if you noticed," he added, triumphantly bringing his speech to a close, "that in the previous chapter I drew your attention to one particular dead young man, and I did this partly for your edification. Suppose he had not yet procreated, had put it off, with the usual argument that there was no rush: he wanted to enjoy being a young warrior, without a child to tie him down. Always the same old refrain: 'There's time.' But as you saw, there wasn't. And the son that he was destined to sire might have been the brilliant doctor who could have prevented a devastating epidemic, or the unbeatable strategist who could have saved his people from invasions, or the spiritual leader who could have given them a reason to go on living. With this potential savior cut down in his prime, the group will die out. The example is crude and simplistic, the strokes are broad, but that is why I think it might just get through to you, my dear Lactarius, and make you see that that no one can go on saying 'there's time' indefinitely. Perhaps it will convince you to stop using your duty to my person as an excuse to put off marrying your girlfriend and becoming a responsible husband and father."

"It's not an excuse, your Excellency. You're always saying you can't live without me."

"But without you to help me, I wouldn't die out; I'm not a population," Fulgentius said before changing the subject.

The following day a dense mist made the landscape elegant, quiet, and calm. The men complained about joint pain caused by the damp. Moving like wooden dolls, they couldn't draw their bows in time when a deer emerged from the white folds billowing beside the path. Their wounded hunters' pride was assuaged by the order that came down the line not to shoot any arrows. Because of the poor visibility, it was unclear how far they were from the city; they might already have entered a zone of pleasure villas, and arrows shot into the mist might have killed ornamental pets or, worse, some wealthy householder.

Towers, burial mounds, and pyramids rose before them suddenly, the whole conglomerate rocking in a hollow of sunlight.
The soldiers' pupils seemed to have taken on a velvety softness
in the mist, and these sharp outlines wounded them almost
like blades. It was early, so they camped. As a rule, the legions
entered cities at evening, when the light was beginning to fail,
so as to hide the signs of fatigue and the vestimentary disorder
resulting from the day's march. It also gave the city time to deck
out the streets to welcome them. This time, in any case, they
used the delay to wash and groom themselves. The Legate was
not able to take part in this hygienic relaxation, since he had to
receive a constant stream of envoys from the city, with or without messages from the authorities.

Finally, as gray dusk fell, the Lupine Legion in all its magnificence marched through the festooned streets to the forum. Carnuntum, the jewel of the plains, had put on its best
to welcome that distillation of imperial power. Famous for its
white roses and its amber trade, the capital of Upper Pannonia
was much smaller inside than out. Its monumental aspect was
a pure illusion, produced by cleverly staggered superimposi-
tions. The columns huddled together; the palaces seemed de-
flated with all their occupants out in the streets to watch the
parade. The fever of welcome was accompanied by the steady
beat of the legionaries' hobnailed sandals marching in time.
The city had six thousand inhabitants, exactly as many as the
men of the Lupine Legion. But this equation proved that num-
bers do not say it all, because the six thousand of the Legion

were all adult men exercising the same profession, while the six thousand of Carnuntum were a blend of the two sexes, and of all ages, conditions, and walks of life.

The official reception, conducted by the governor with his consuls and praetors and their respective wives, took place in the Forum. From there they proceeded to the temple of Venus to make offerings, a formality that the Legate endured with a stony face, repressing yawns. Like most of his colleagues, he upheld the importance of maintaining the ancestral ceremonies but he could hardly fail to see the childishness of those tales about the gods.

Night had fallen by the time they came out. The soldiers had left earlier for the field on the outskirts where they were to camp. All the city's hetaerae had set off in the same direction. Although Fulgentius was quite happy to pitch his tent among his men, on this occasion he accepted the lodgings prepared for him in the governor's palace, leaving Lactarius to act as liaison. The following day, as a sign of good will, he submitted to the orgies, the din of plectra, and the feasts, as if to get his social obligations over and done with. After that, he would be free to interview the actors he had identified by means of discreet inquiries and had informed of his impending visit. He sacrificed a day but no more; each hour not spent in rehearsals was a lost hour that would lodge itself in the performance.

ON THE MORNING OF THE SECOND DAY, AS ARRANGED, Fulgentius went to meet the actors, who were waiting for him at the temple of Venus. They took him to one of the little chambers at the back. That, they explained, was where they rehearsed, sewed their costumes, gilded their masks, adjusted their megaphones, and generally got themselves ready. The amphitheater where they performed was not far away (they offered to give him a tour that afternoon), but it was a primitive arena, without amenities; they only went there for the performances, or for the dress rehearsal, so they had set themselves up in the temple, with the blessing of the presiding priestess, who was also one of the actresses. "We have already met," said Fulgentius, referring to the ceremony on the day of his arrival, and greeting the old vestal virgin with a stiff bow. The dozen actors were, on the whole, rather mature, indeed verging on senescence. This implied experience and responsibility, but also weariness and detachment. The author was already beginning to miss the ardor of a young cast. But he was in two minds because he felt it might be interesting to see his headlong, passionate tragedy performed by a troupe of creaky veterans.

The director of the company, however, was young. A freed slave by the name of Julius, he dominated the meeting. Already informed of the Legate's plans, he thanked him effusively. They were honored to receive his trust, although as Carnuntum's only theater company, he added, they had no reason to feel that they had been preferred. But it was still an honor to have been entrusted with his play, which would be a welcome addition to the dusty old repertoire that they had relied on for longer than anyone could remember. Julius said how excited he had been the previous day to discover that the general was the author of a tragedy. The fact that the work had not emerged from the stale and stuffy world of professional drama was in itself a promise of freshness and originality. The director was champing at the bit, and hoped that he would be equal to the task.

Having delivered this conventional speech, Julius spread out a scroll and proceeded as if by magic to offer intelligent observations. It had not escaped him, for a start, that the protagonist shared his name with the author. "A coincidence?" he asked. "Or was there a deliberate autobiographical intention?"

"I wouldn't say deliberate; no forethought went into this product of my ... youth." Fulgentius didn't want to say "childhood," although it would have been closer to the truth. "But yes, the protagonist is me."

"An autobiographical tragedy ... I've never heard of such a thing. Are there any precedents?"

"Not that I know."

"A magnificent display of originality."

"I wasn't trying to be original. That's just the way it came out."

"How many works do you have to your credit?"

"This is it. It's the only one I've written."

"That's unusual too. It demonstrates a further degree of originality, I would say. And a laudable thrift, when so many are incurably prolific."

"I think your two questions answer each other," said the Legate after a moment's reflection. "My tragedy is autobiographical because it is unique, and unique because it is autobiographical. In recounting my one and only life, I exhausted the genre that I had invented. I could have moved on to other themes, but I felt no inner need to write more, and whatever is written without that need, which I would call visceral, is bound to sound hollow or as if it was written solely to fulfill a professional duty. By profession I am a soldier, a general in the glorious Roman army. As a playwright, I think of myself as a sublime amateur."

The freed slave scanned the manuscript with a schooled eye. On reaching the end, he made the inevitable remark about the autobiographical license of killing off the author-protagonist.

Fulgentius replied that he had simply obeyed the iron law of the tragic genre, which required there to be a poignant finale. And what could be more poignant than death? He remembered with a smile that he had written the scene mechanically, in his role as "tragic author," and only when he had finished did he realize that the death he had versified was his own.

The meeting had gone well but it ended on a worrying note, when the freed slave announced that he would be playing the lead role. It made sense; there were no other serious contenders. Julius was the only actor in his prime; he had a fine presence, a good voice, and obvious dramatic talent ... But his effeminate nature was no less obvious. In real life, Fulgentius had nothing against sodomy. The soldier's life, with its long periods of exclusively masculine cohabitation, would have broadened any mind. But it was different in fiction. Thinking about it was like being drawn into an accelerating vortex. He was about to say something, but just before he opened his mouth, the thought occurred to him that this Julius might actually be a woman posing as a man.

With a sigh of stifled despair, he resigned himself to his fate. He didn't inquire any further; it was a way of protecting himself. But there was one more thing he had to know because it was essential: how long the preparation would take. With his ladylike manners, Julius-Julia declared that they would start studying the text immediately and distributing the roles ... Fulgentius interrupted, insisting that time was of the essence. He pretended that his men were impatient to scale the Carpathians, that the threat of the rebel tribes would not allow for any delay ... Letting his natural eloquence carry him away, he said that it was preferable, from his point of view, to take the plunge after just a few rehearsals; it wouldn't matter too much if it was still a bit rough around the edges; excessive memorizing and preparation could give the production a mechanical feel; vitality, in theater, took the form of imperfection.

The sole purpose of this theory, which he had made up on the spot, was to accelerate the proceedings, which had begun to fill him with a secret dread. And whether or not he managed to convince the actors, seven days later they were ready for the première. At which point Fulgentius had something resembling a panic attack. He had spent the week trying to think of other things but realized that had failed utterly, however much attention he had paid to the feasts, the coursing of oryx, the statuary, and the fish farms. When the moment came, all the apprehensions that he had tried to repress rose up and overwhelmed him. What if he was faced with an effete Fulgentius on stage, loading each line with innuendo and distorting the overall meaning of the tragedy? He wasn't so worried about what other people might think: he was afraid that he wouldn't be able to empathize with himself as a character. Nothing else mattered. That identification had become a vital elixir; he almost believed that without it, he wouldn't be able to go on living.

And yet the thought of skipping the performance didn't even cross his mind. He put off the impulse to escape, diverting it to the following day. He ordered his men to strike camp and prepare to set off before dawn. That would give him an excuse to leave as soon as the play was over, and avoid the obligation to comment and explain, which might have been awkward if his nightmare came true. To take offense at his sudden departure would have been unreasonable, since the general was doing what he always did: the time spent in a city was determined by how long it took the local actors to stage his play, and he always left immediately after the performance.

The cream of Carnuntum society was present in the amphitheater. From the opening speeches and the introductory tirade in which the protagonist cursed the fate that obliged him to go to war, the real-life Fulgentius sitting in the fourth row forgot all his apprehensions and entered wholeheartedly into the charmed circle of the fiction. Julius was giving the character a consistency that no other actor had achieved or even attempted. His effeminacy, toned down just a little for the stage, endowed this general torn between manliness and survival with a touching fragility. When Fulgentius recited the lines to himself in time with Julius, it wasn't the simple identification of a naive spectator but the superidentification of souls in a state of plasticity.

In preparatory meetings Fulgentius generally avoided striking up a conversation with the actor who was to play his role: he worried that getting to know the person might prevent him from seeing the character on stage and deprive him of the pleasure of complete identification. This time he had recklessly spoken with Julius, who was present (too present) in his thoughts. And yet what he found was that far from interfering with the identification, familiarity enriched it. Still, he wasn't rushing to general conclusions; it might have been a one-off effect, favored by the double nature of Julius-Julia.

The performance was a total success, at least for Fulgentius. The old-timers who made up the rest of the cast, with their shaky voices and arthritic movements, formed the perfect backdrop to the one-man drama. They created a posthumous atmosphere, which intensified the strangeness. It was clear from the cautious comments of other spectators afterwards that the general had been the only one to appreciate that strangeness as art. It may have been a product of chance but it was art nonetheless.

In any case he sought neither comments nor praise. He never did. Sycophants had a very limited repertoire, which he already knew by heart. On this occasion he also feared that trite compliments might dull the keen singularity of his emotional response. He was crossing the atrium and had almost managed to slip away when a familiar face appeared before him, one he would never have expected to encounter there, so far from Rome. It was Aeneas Septimio, a consul known for his participation in the Claudian Reforms, disgraced and exiled to remote Carnuntum. Fulgentius, who paid no attention to politics, had been unaware of the consul's exile; it was news to him, but years old, to judge from the look of poor Aeneas. The man was a physical wreck. He must have been one of those Romans for whom there was nothing worth knowing beyond the agoras of the capital with their rumor mills and power games, one of those who must consume that slime to sustain their interest in life. That limitation cost them dearly. Transplanted elsewhere, they shriveled like weeds in winter. The founding fathers must have had the measure of that sort of man when they decided on exile as the supreme punishment. This specimen was a veritable ghost of his former self. If his aim was to inspire pity, he was succeeding, although not as he would have liked. This was not the first time in the course of the Legate's travels that an exile had come to court his favor, so he wasn't taken by surprise. He had no idea how much influence he might have on the

imperial authorities when it came to interceding on behalf of
an offender and no intention of finding out. He had perfected
an infallible technique for getting rid of this sort of petitioner
without committing himself: let the man talk on and on until,
running out of things to say, he began to repeat and contradict
himself and finally beat an embarrassed retreat without having
received any kind of promise.

This episode gave Fulgentius food for thought. He was
shocked by the supplicant's lack of psychological insight or
shrewdness. Hadn't he been among the spectators? Given his
condition, he would not have dared to ask for a formal audience, so the only way to get a hearing was to intercept the general on his way out of the amphitheater. To have done that, he
must have seen the play, and discovered that Fulgentius was the
author. Didn't he know that vanity ruled in the field of artistic
creation? Could he really have been so naive? With a pair of
well placed compliments, he could have secured the good will
that he so badly needed. How hard could that have been, even
if he had to lie? But no. He asked for something, without giving anything in return. And to have done it just then, minutes
after the end of the play, was almost insulting. No, Fulgentius
was damned if he was going to help him.

Following the drift of these thoughts, the general imagined
how he would have gone about it. He was at an advantage, of
course, because he knew what it was like to be on the other
side of the altar, receiving the sacrifice. How simple it would
have been for him to win the favor of an artist who could have

helped him in some way. How easy to turn a compliment that sounded intelligent and sincere, even (or especially) if it were neither one nor the other. Writers, he had observed (and this resonated with the writer in him), were prone to the belief that no one grasped the deep intentions of their works. So when they came across someone who might, just might, have been their dreamed-of ideal reader, they clung to that person more tightly than to a spouse or a fortune. Anxiety and hope made them easy prey for those who knew which buttons to push.

But these musings left the general feeling less pleased than he might have hoped. He looked into his heart and saw an abyss of hypocrisy. After all, Aeneas had demonstrated a scrupulous honesty in making his request without attempting to sweeten the pill. What courage it must have taken to do something like that! True, but even so, Fulgentius would have preferred some guile.

AT THE FOOT OF THE GIGANTIC CARPATHIANS, THE Legate gathered all his centurions to inform them of what he had heard in Carnuntum. It wasn't solid or trustworthy intelligence, far from it: fear, fermenting in ignorance, had made chimeras to measure for each mind, which is to say they were generally vast, since people tend to fear the large rather than the small, except when they're trying to be subtle. It was as if the centurions were about to enter a subjective realm. But exaggerations were always based on something real: that was built into the very definition of the verb *to exaggerate*. What Fulgentius had to do in addressing his officers was translate those flourishes of terror into concrete information, which was scarce: monks were refusing to pay taxes, supposedly at the behest of their gods and their sometime allies the Carian counts (in whose territory not a few renegade Romans had gone into hiding, setting up tin-pot nations in caves). As intelligence went, this was both too much and not enough. Like dreams, these descriptions were made up of familiar elements recombined to produce a new result. The process was more mechanical than creative, and ended up devaluing the unknown.

Fulgentius felt that it would be wise to warn his men about the rebel monks. He told them not to extrapolate from their own idea of religion, based on the Graeco-Roman cults: an elegant, literary system of practices, which spoke to the intellect, and was primarily a provider of content for art and ceremony. He couldn't be entirely sure about what they would soon encounter because he was extrapolating too, but he said that it had more to do with the blind instincts of animals in a world where life was cheap, since all value resided in the powers of nature. (Conceiving of a supernatural realm would have required the use of a brain, the organ that can also explain how such a realm is a fiction created to entertain and instruct). He laid it on with a trowel, adding gruesome details as if for the sake of realism, and was very satisfied with the long faces of his listeners.

What happened once they got into the mountains contradicted each and every word he had said, inevitably, since facts are not words. Nights and days followed one another, always similar but never exactly the same. The sense of being on a journey deepened, and the men felt a vague compulsion to make the most of it. Having abandoned the peaceable routines of home, they naturally wanted to take something to compensate for the trials and hardships of an expedition in the wilderness. And since for the moment there were no material spoils to be taken, all that remained was thought: the spontaneous ideas from which they might draw interesting conclusions. What a true blessing, reflected the Legate, that thought and the words that conveyed it went everywhere with the thinker, weighed nothing, and were always available.

He tried out this idea on Lactarius, who was always on hand for his experiments in communication.

"Tell me, Lactarius, have you ever felt that you are a man?"

"A man, your Excellency? I'm only an assistant."

"What I mean is, have you ever felt that you are free to do exactly what you want, as if you were the only man in the world?"

"But if there was nobody else, I wouldn't be able to do anything to anyone."

"True. I hadn't thought of that. Or rather, I didn't express myself well. Suppose you were the only real man, and all the others were insubstantial simulacra."

"Isn't that how we normally function?"

The young man's clever rejoinder was greeted by a hearty laugh, the laugh of a patrician with consuls in his family tree. Freedom implied contempt of one's neighbor.

"To change the subject: have you ever experienced an earthquake?"

"No."

"Would an earthquake seen far away look different from one seen close up?"

" . . . "

"Or to go a step further, suppose there is a fire in the Forum, or an earthquake that topples its columns and pediments, and the next day, contemplating the ruins, you ask the obvious question: Is it worth rebuilding? How would you answer?"

Heartily fed up with being subjected to these rather silly and mostly gratuitous digressions, Lactarius used some maintenance task as an excuse to slip away into the ranks. Fulgentius went on talking to himself. It was better that way: he could range more freely in his observations. And he didn't have to worry about pitching his discourse at a level that would suit his interlocutor; he could keep taking it up to the next level and go as high as he liked. As the days went by, he came to realize that the journey did not have to be purely functional, a method of reaching an end point that rendered the route dispensable (or forgettable, like a night of sleep between two days). This prompted him to pay more attention to things as they appeared along the way and to draw conclusions that enriched the life of his conscious mind. One such thought concerned the rivers, which until then he had regarded merely as obstacles or con-firmations of a wandering line on one of the dubious maps. For almost all of his life, Fulgentius had been the sort of distracted traveler to whom all rivers look alike, distinguished only by how hard or easy they are to cross. An unforgivable blindness, when the river before him now was making such a persuasive and even poignant show of its individuality.

It was an old river, hauling its pale waters wearily with an ailing grumble, so slowly that it sometimes seemed to have stopped, as if it had given up its efforts to pursue a journey that had come to seem futile. Its waves were wrinkled and scat-tered with rubbish, collapsing sadly onto each other, as if to say, "Come on, we can still do it," but in a tone of voice that left no doubt: in fact, they couldn't and if they were persisting it was only by a force of habit that had already begun to fail.

The meaning of this spectacle was revealed in full when Fulgentius observed another river, not far away. This one was young and behaved like a child: it leaped and ran, giggled and

chortled, splashing out in all directions, making bubbles for the
sheer fun of it. Transient rainbows thrived on its vapors, linking
their curves in a joyful dance. The river's plump body was made
of the purest, most virginal, and transparent water. It had energy to spare, which it channeled into somersaults and sprints.
The sight of it kindled affection and joy, but one couldn't help
remembering the other river and thinking of time's cruel power.

The analogy was self-evident: old age and youth. Fulgentius
had once been that young river, all vitality and drive, preserving
the child within, and the child between his legs, who had grown
along with him. Energy and the pleasure of spending it were
blended in this metaphor: as the river was the image of life, the
child who stood up on his own was the image of his genitality,
and in both cases it was a joyful liquid emission that gave meaning to existence. This was all well and good, but there was also
the other river with its moribund whispers to remind him that
he was older than his parents and grandparents had been when
they died and that his military and social achievements could
never make up for the white hair, the wrinkles, and the rheu-
matic aches. Thus the allegory played itself out.

When Fulgentius realized what he was doing, he reacted:
what was the point of that intellectual exercise? It wouldn't
yield any knowledge that he could use or display. All it could
do was depress him. In that case, it was better to go through
life without noticing anything at all. The problem (why it had
taken him so long to see it he couldn't understand) must have
been that those reflections partook of what he hated most in

the world: philosophy. He had started off well, with an implicit—implicitly poetic—description of the rivers, but then he had strayed in the direction of poetry's polar opposite.

To reverse this drift, not without effort, since that wretch philosophy was diabolically skilled at infiltrating the brain's staunchest defenses, he set himself containment exercises. One was to attribute an imaginary life to the mountains that appeared along the way, in the distance or nearby. If he saw two of different sizes close together, he pretended that the bigger one was the father and the smaller one his son, and then invented a conversation between them. The son, for example, asked his father for a few sesterces to go out on the town, only to be turned away with the irrefutable argument that since he was a mountain he wouldn't be going anywhere.

Fulgentius was so pleased to have come up with this unexpected punchline that he burst out laughing, startling Lactarius, who having seen him riding quietly had returned to his side. The general immediately began to invent what his faithful assistant might have been thinking: "How can this old crackpot be in charge of so many fighting men?" Except—and this was the funniest part—it wasn't an invention, because that's what Lactarius was actually thinking, as he confirmed with the following question:

"Forgive my curiosity, your Excellency, but how did you come to be a general?"

"I'll tell you the story. It's well worth the telling: the sort of thing that only happens once in a lifetime. In spite of which,

I've never told anyone, because I don't want it getting back to my wife, and it's a reasonable fear because, as you'll see, this is the kind of story that provokes an irresistible desire to tell it to someone else in turn, so there's no knowing how far it might spread."

"You can rely on my discretion, your Excellency."

"It's not a question of reliability. I feel as if I had dreamed you up to be the hearer of this episode, which is so central to my career, and once that purpose is fulfilled, you will vanish into thin air as if you had never existed."

After this enigmatic and vaguely threatening introduction, ignoring the frightened look on the face of his young assistant, Fulgentius launched into the following story:

"Once, many years ago, I had intimate relations with a pretty young woman I had met a few hours earlier. In the legion to which I belonged at the time, this sort of thing was fairly common on long campaigns. In other circumstances it might have been a cause for surprise, since she was young enough to be my daughter (although I was still in my prime) and had the bearing and beauty of a queen, while I was a simple centurion. I could only thank my lucky stars and the legionary's appeal in the eyes of naive provincial girls. This one wasn't so naive, as demonstrated by her exploits on the palliasse that served me as a bed. I matched her zest. She inspired me; I was more active than usual. Much more, to tell the truth. Incomparably more. I was like another man, and yet I rediscovered myself in this new and limitless virility. The world had never seen such embraces:

we melted into puddles of golden sweat, slid ardently over each other's bodies. My emissions were torrential, but far from sapping my timely engorgement, they revived it. I was iron, she a warm mass shot through with shudders. Our kisses were souls, our caresses tales of the end of the world and its consequent starting over. Despite the lexical wealth of our language, I could find no words to describe the smoothness of her skin or the curve of her haunch when she collapsed face down beside me. It was one of those situations in which you hardly believe that something so good is actually happening, but you have to yield to the evidence and admit that it's real, and then comes a twinge of melancholy, because reality is successive, and each episode must come to an end to make way for the next. With another, deeper kiss, and another tumble, which revealed new surfaces of her splendid volume, she lifted me into a new empyrean. I thrilled to her lips more than anything; I wanted to go on devouring them forever. I can't call it love, because it was pure, unadulterated sex, although maybe I was under the sway of the dictum I always repeat to my friends: 'I can't imagine sex without love.' Why the hell not? But maybe it's true. In any case, this attraction transcended the act, and I gave myself to it body and soul. Once again, my kisses descended to her breasts, her divine navel, and that wellspring of hidden sweetness, where my tongue sought out the elusive source ... I won't go on; I don't want to provoke a reaction that, given the rigidity of your laminar cuirass, might prove to be most uncomfortable. But I think I've conveyed the idea, while treating myself to the pleasure of using words to relive an experience that was beyond the reach of words.

"The next day I woke up with a terrible pain in the lower abdomen. I ruled out indigestion because I hadn't eaten anything. I thought of my recent amatory feats but ruled them out too, because if I set a precedent in that area I could end up never having sex again. Then I simply ruled out everything because the effects that I was suffering were beyond any possible cause. The torture was intense. It made me howl. It was as if molten iron were being stirred up and brought to the boil in my pelvic cavity. My hip bones had turned into pincers, squeezing until I convulsed. My testes were two balls of fire. My bowels a long path of spasms and cramps that made me thrash and toss. My member, reduced to its minimal dimensions, attained its maximal capacity for pain. I thought my time had come. What was I being punished for? The pain was mounting relentlessly. It was clear that this ascent could not lead to anything good. I was on the point of fainting when a different sensation made itself felt: something was coming out down there. The process was long and difficult: the pain soared to a paroxysm but then at once began to relent, and I realized with a mixture of stupor and joy that what was coming out was my new self, myself as a Roman general. Suddenly it all became clear: the pains that I had suffered were those of a peculiar labor. I had been impregnated by the Goddess, who had temporarily taken the form of one of those girls who know how to make a man happy. And that is how I was promoted to the rank of general."

Lactarius was riding in silence. All the others were silent too: six thousand oversized children, before whom local civilizations collapsed, leaving mysterious debris. Although Fulgentius was endlessly distracted by his ad hoc dialectics, he had to take the landscape into account. Not only as a source of themes but also as something he had to pass through: no simple task. A wretched topography raised barriers of rock and abyss, enveloped in fog. For a traveler in reasonable physical shape without heavy luggage, it wouldn't have been too hard. But with a legion to lug ... The precipices piled up, multiplying their effects. Walls of pink basalt, covered with an impalpable down, held up the march for long days at a time, before finally seeing fit to open their doors. In the valleys, which might have afforded some respite, the men had to wade across great silvery expanses of floodwater. Thorns gave out only to be replaced by nocturnal mosses; the angles of the moonlight made everything stranger; the winds howled, and the sun dazzled. Looking down from the heights, vision was defeated by the universal collapsing of space. A little higher still, when they felt they were already touching the clouds, they came to the crater of a volcano and circled its rim, gazing down at the crimson boiling lava: any one of its bubbles would have been large enough to swallow the Coliseum. But a spill sent them fleeing down slopes of pure petrified turbulence, and then it took days of worrying and counting to reassemble the scattered troops. On they went, marching along devious cornices, over solitary saddles. The crags loomed like colossal doves; the broken schists broke all over again. How strange it was, they thought, to be surrounded by large-scale chaos while everything at the small scale was in perfect order, as they were able to confirm by examining the eyes of flies, the scales of lizards, and the petals of the violet. And if these relatively small things were so well ordered, what must it have been like at the scale of the truly tiny, the most deeply hidden: the atoms of Lucretius. The storms came crashing down from the peaks; black clouds full of lightning bounced off the slopes. The thunderbolts sent trees and men flying. The landscape, flipped upside down, sizzled as if full of crickets, and was caught in its fall by the arm of a giant. In the subsequent calm, eagles took flight in the canyons, effortlessly riding the updrafts, followed by the gazes of the men, until they seemed to brush the vault of heaven, visible between the peaks. The legionaries had to respect the traffic of the mountains: their great standstills and ancient convulsions. To enter into the spectacle of nature, even the forbidding nature of a hard-edged mountain range, was to alter it, shifting its specific gravity, transferring its colors to the field of ideas. The legion clung to the walls and columns of this rugged, pre-Roman, universal realm. As for Fulgentius, like an artist disappointed by his efforts to bring life to the inanimate, although there was no more that he could have done, he wondered quizzically why it was that he always ended up with fragments of a world, never worlds in their entirety.

BEYOND A CERTAIN WOOD, THEY WERE ACCOMPANIED by wolves. The standard-bearers paid their respects by donning the wolf's-head caps that they wore for public parades, manifesting the Lupine Legion's totemic identification with the proud terrors of the north. The wolves marched along with the men but kept their distance. Magnificent creatures with dark coats, flaming eyes, and a spring in their step, they gave off an ancestral silence that permeated the ranks of the boisterous legionaries, who in this rapport with the wolf recovered the prestige of the invincible. The mutual respect of man and beast was based on the eternal youth of both collectivities. The bronze Capitoline Wolf engendered soldiers to renew the ranks, just as the pack's fine specimens were born of wild couplings in the woods. Never domesticated, and practicing a refined savagery that placed them at the top of the food chain, the wolves were men to wolves. They reminded man of his regal destiny, the transhuman continuity of his rule. At night, the king of the wolves marked his inviolable domain with a solitary howl, a cadenza echoing on and on to proclaim that they were still there, the representatives, along with what they represented. The beasts kept watch, mounted guard, and nothing escaped the gaze of their yellow eyes, which could see as well in the dark as in broad daylight, thanks to the *tapetum lucidum* behind the retina.

The action began when the legionaries reached the table-lands. But the hostility they encountered up there was eclipsed by their bewilderment: they couldn't believe there were people with an outlook so different from their own. As part of an empire that spanned the world, they were the ones who got to impose norms of behavior and thought. Understanding the causal chains that shaped reality had cost them centuries of work, which had consisted basically of annihilating anything that was different. So when they came across difference once again, it was an encounter with the past. Not that they had much opportunity for comparative studies: the resistance they met, which was active and resolute unto death, forced them to employ certain radical strategies that they had kept in reserve until then. Their victory was assured in advance, they had no doubts about that; the problem was how to achieve it. For the first time in the campaign, they had to engage in real combat, rather than simply killing unarmed civilians as an example and a warning. That had been part of a language of deeds, but words could not survive on the tablelands, and action referred only to action itself. Which was paradoxical, because what really counted there was symbolic and grounded in religion.

The bewilderment of the men throughout this whole episode was due in part to the remedies they had to take for altitude sickness. The rarefied air caused dizziness and double vision. To counteract these symptoms they chewed vasodilating stems. The treatment worked but had marked side effects, which turned out to be useful as they all intensified ferocity. When the men put the stems in their mouths, they were transformed from Romans into bloodthirsty satyrs. Some hallucinated and flung away their spears and shields, convinced that their bare hands were enough. The centurions (who had taken double doses) did nothing to stop them, since madness was no disadvantage in war.

The legionaries pitted chaos against control. The monks' troops seemed to be receiving telepathic orders. They weren't, of course, there was nothing supernatural going on: it was that delayed telepathy, so common in archaic communities. In this case, hypnotic mastery of the will was facilitated by superstition. From temples clinging to the mountain heights, stone forts without doors or windows, the monks issued orders that were obeyed with no regard for death. The legion had to battle for each parcel of land, spattering the black stone with the blood of fanatics. Sheltering beneath their shields, which formed a sort of mobile roof, the units of spearmen climbed up marmot tracks. Having eaten nothing but carrots since the beginning of the weeklong battle, they feasted in imagination on the cakes and liqueurs of the monkish cellars. Their ghostly foes, armed with bronze axes, wore dark tunics and red bonnets. They screamed as if possessed, invoking gods about which they had the simplest of theological notions.

Although impatient to make the ascent, Fulgentius followed the action with great interest from a comfortable fireside at the foot of the bluff. His assistant, Lactarius, whose eyes were sharper, pointed out details, and he was aided in turn by the slave boy, who could see a fly on the horizon. (Not that there was much of a horizon, with all those escarpments). Eventually someone came down to tell the general that they had captured a temple.

The monks had fled like rats when they had seen their last defenses giving way. But some had fallen into the hands of the invaders, who simply by applying psychological pressure had obtained all the information they needed. The terror the monks inspired in the local population had been due to their invisibility; when the veil fell away, they were revealed as physically and mentally fragile, small men with voices grown soft and lungs exhausted by all that blowing of long horns. It emerged from their confessions that there were some forty temples, all under the authority of the ceremonial complex on the highest peak.

The number came as something of a blow to morale, but the Legate had no trouble convincing his officers that if they showed their resolve and headed straight for the system's nerve center, the resistance would collapse all at once. He opened the monk hunt immediately, and when his men had dragged three hundred from the mountain clefts, they crucified them on the most conspicuous hilltop they could find and left the corpses hanging there. It soon became clear that the message had been received in temples farther afield: one by one the long horns began to sound. Without the echoes, they would have been impotent. The players drew cries from far-off rock faces, using sonic

maps that were a part of their esoteric knowledge. What the naive mountain dwellers heard as a call from the beyond was simply, for the men of the legion, an exotic musical performance.

The sound did not even disturb their sleep, for the horn
blasts were muffled by the thick stone walls of the temple they
had occupied, having thrown out the monks; and they paid no
attention, in any case—there was so much inside to discover
and plunder. Fulgentius toured the rooms with a connoisseur's
eye, making a mental note of each god, each carved plinth and
capital. There were deities with antlers, ancient saints with large
wooden feet, but not a single goddess, a sure sign of blind bar-
barity. As the legionaries had presumed, the pantries were well
stocked. There wasn't enough to feed them all, but they made a
hecatomb of the sacred goats, roasting them merrily on the terraces. The stars, seen from there, were blindingly bright: rivers
and seas of heavenly bodies set in the black of the universe.

They waited two more days before the final assault. The intimidation had worked, provoking a comprehensive rout, and
they met almost no resistance in the climb to the Great Temple,
whose doors swung open before them. The hierarchy of living
gods and high priests had remained at their posts, resigned to
laying their idols down before the eagles of Rome. Fulgentius
discharged his official duties as quickly as he could: he questioned the prisoners about the functioning of the mystical
state, sent armed detachments to the nearby temples with the
message that their deities had been taken hostage, examined
the accounts with the help of expert readers, locked the liv-

ing gods in a tower, put them on a diet of bread and water, and shared out their thousands of nubile wives for the amusement of the troops. More than these tasks, what interested Fulgentius was thoroughly exploring the monstrous edifice of which he was now the lord and master.

The Great Temple's various intersecting levels were modeled on but also modified the relief of the peak to which they clung. There were hundreds of rooms, from little chambers ideal for moments of unplanned intimacy, to the monumental reception halls, in which a herd of elephants might have romped. The design was like nothing Fulgentius had ever seen: curved walls, diagonal columns, arches whose span defied geometry, onyx floors displaying an upside-down reality in the depths of their transparent darkness. The rarest materials were combined in the ceilings. The walls were covered with paintings of apocalyptic scenes, apparently suited to the sensual appetites of that mountain race. The furniture was inexhaustibly rich in details; each stool seemed to have required a hundred years of incising with a golden needle point. The delicate clusters of crystal, the mercury-glass door handles, the mother of pearl, and the little quartz almonds: everything was oval-shaped, and the rough soldiers, inured to austerity, gaped at it all in amazement. Knowing that the temple had housed one or two thousand monks, plus their concubines and servants, Fulgentius wondered how they had been able to move, given the enormous number of statues. The building seemed to have been made for these sculptures, which were perfectly at ease, displaying their demonic faces stupefied by immobility. Rivers of gems had been poured over them.

Admiration halted at the threshold of beauty, detained by critical scruples. One of these resulted from the encounter between unverifiable, supernatural claims and a mind nourished by reality. The religious masquerade with its painted effigies could not hide the trickery, the scheming, and the will to power. And this led to a more radical rejection, prompted by the sight of wealth accumulating for no purpose other than display, at the expense of a fairer distribution of income. In every corner of that endless labyrinth of galleries and rooms, there were luxury items worth enough to sustain whole villages for years. Historically, it made no sense; that was why it was justified by reference to theological eternities. Fulgentius was not impermeable to this reasoning, but true to an ingrained mental quirk, he transposed it immediately from the muddy terrain of ethics, where he was careful never to tread, to the iridescent expanse of aesthetics, where Evil was simply one color among many. If those stupid shepherds let the monks exploit them, that was their problem; it made no difference to him. He was even inclined to give religion some credit: after all, it produced more art than politics did.

These reflections, along with what emerged from two meetings of the general staff and the examination of the temple accounts, inspired the proclamation that Lactarius wrote out on the general's instructions, copies of which were distributed before the legion's departure.

"We leave you with the strong recommendation to pay the taxes promptly, in gold, which is legal tender and abundantly to be found in the bowels of these mountains. The slaves who work the mines are compelled by the magical arts that you have practiced from time immemorial. Don't think we don't know! And don't think for a moment that you can fool Romans with tricks like that. If we let you play them, it is only because we are doing the same, except that our magic is the invincible power of the legions. Be warned: if you fail to pay the annual, biannual, and triannual tributes on time, we shall unleash upon you all the destructive fury in our power, and reduce your stone gods to impalpable dust."

A postdatum indicated that the Carian counts, whose pasturelands stretched away to the east, would be responsible for collecting the tributes. This was a stroke of genius on the part of Fulgentius, ensuring peace with the Carians, who would be glad of the chance to siphon off as much of the funds as they could, and would therefore do whatever it took to make the monks pay up. As the Legate explained to Lactarius, it was worth letting them take a little cut, if it meant the bulk of the loot was secure. Peace came at a price, as opposed to war, which was free.

The legionaries began their descent, preceded by the news that they had pacified the region. Golden autumn had reached its apogee, rich in visions. The ceaseless migration of birds overhead was accompanied on the ground by stampedes of deer and wild boar fleeing before the hunters. Colonies of small black birds roosting in the cedar tops set the branches quivering as if in a private wind. Over it all, rainbows presided, lingering after sunset. By day, the men were dazzled by the sun off the quartz; by night, phosphenes danced in their eyes. They took the weight off their feet, which the vastness of the empire had punished, and idled the daylight hours away. They cast dice listlessly onto their shields. The clicking sound of bone on metal elicited dreamlike thoughts. The region's typical marshes, where their eyes went fishing, stretched away like inland seas. They witnessed the creation of swans on the lakes and the boldness of the wildcats among the fumaroles.

FOR A TIME THERE WAS A FEELING AMONG THE LEG-ate's entourage that their work was done and hostilities had ceased. Nobody said it aloud, which spared them having to eat their words when the hail of arrows resumed. The teeming Rhaetian battalions fell upon them: shaggy, well-fed barbarians, fiercely defending the rock valves at the heart of Pannonia. Purple flames leaped back and forth; the price of victory rose and fell. The legion conquered territory inch by inch. Being an invincible corps, it prevailed by virtue of its mere reality, and yet reality prevailed over the legionaries in turn, constantly forcing them into positions that put their invincibility at risk. It was a hazardous and hectic time: battling all day, capturing villages, suicidal horsemen attacking by moonlight, supplies running short (the men tearing weeds from the cliffs to eat), makeshift hospitals, and all this after having been born with silver spoons in their mouths. The din of arms responded to the war cries of the natives, who were ready to die in defense of their freedom. There was no alternative: they would have to be forcibly taught the duties of subordination.

The legionaries had all come to resemble one another. Not only in the way they dressed—they took punctilious care of their uniforms—but in everything else as well: haircut, expression, gait, the shape of the mouth when pronouncing the liquid

consonants of Latin, everything, in short, that could be trans-
mitted by a long and intimate coexistence, and by the natural-
ization of trust among men whose lives were in one another's
hands day after day. This undifferentiated mass passed through
territories where settlement, migration, and interbreeding had
produced diverse populations; it made the Romans feel alone,
tightly locked into their identity, up against a world whose form
and content changed with every step they took.

Surrounded by the clamor of battle with its shouts and
sneezes, busy sending detachments in one direction or another, counting the dead, ordering more axes, Fulgentius could
hardly believe that there were people who traveled for pleasure. In general, those diligent hedonists spoke not of pleasure
but of broadening their horizons, escaping from that insidious
form of provincialism that thrived in the world's most important city. They often resorted to a cliché when weighing up
their experiences or giving advice: Rome was good for culture,
the provinces for nature. As a sworn enemy of clichés, Fulgentius was inclined to argue for the opposite position, on the
grounds that culture only comes into its own when grounded
in plurality. The Roman culture that his tutor had so proudly
extolled—unique, monolithic, and determined to destroy all
potential rivals—was actually a kind of nature. In the infinite
provincial expanses, on the other hand, diverse cultures flourished and coexisted, and one of their many achievements had
been to master the forging of iron, which allowed the people to
make weapons and rise up against the central power that was

attempting to impose its culture on them. And this, in turn, had led to the general being sent to pacify them by force.

With all that was going on, it is hard to imagine how General Fulgentius could have been upset by something entirely unrelated. War trivializes all other sources of preoccupation. And yet his soul was elastic enough to make room for one more worry. It was conveyed to him by an emissary who had come directly from Rome with a letter. When the messenger's arrival was announced, Fulgentius thought it must be an official communiqué from the Senate, and quickly ran through all the possible instructions that it might have contained. So he was more than a little surprised to discover, when the envelope reached his hands, that the sender was his administrator and biographer Claudius Marius Resus. Surprise soon gave way to alarm. The enormous cost of sending an emissary half way across the empire could only be justified by a message of the utmost importance or urgency. Since it had come from the man who had control of his treasury and knew the full story of his life, there was reason to be apprehensive. A drop in the value of the metal that his savings were invested in? The illegal occupation of his country villa? His slaves carried off by a plague? These old and new fears, carefully archived in his waking mind as well as in his nightmares, paraded before him in order. And there were further reasons to be worried: all the possible threats to the wellbeing of family members, or dark secrets from his past that might have come to light ... He realized eventually that it would be better to stop speculating and read the actual letter.

What it said, essentially, was that his little grandson had a cough, that was all. Incredulity set his head spinning. He didn't know where to begin not being able to believe it. He did have a grandson who was about to turn two. Bearing that fact in mind, he read the letter again. When it came to setting things out clearly, Claudius Marius had never been a shining example. The message was clear enough, nevertheless. Fulgentius deciphered it little by little, gathering the scattered fragments of information and putting them in order. The child had woken with a dry cough, which had to be watched in case it developed into a worrying illness. The task could not be left to slaves, who were clumsy, ignorant, and fundamentally indifferent to the wellbeing of the families they served. The little boy's grandmother had been obliged to step in. There followed an encomium of that saintly woman, who embodied all the virtues of the traditional Roman matron, the pride of her household gods. The author of the missive had allowed himself to be carried away by an enthusiastic admiration that was totally out of place. Fulgentius felt a twitch of annoyance. Who had authorized his administrator to interfere in family matters and be so rude to his employer? He had overstepped his brief. He was also a biographer, of course, and as such he had gathered information from the general's family and friends. It had been a mistake to entrust one man with two largely incompatible tasks. A mistake it was now too late to correct, because with everything Claudius knew about his employer's possessions and his past, he could be a dangerous blackmailer if he were dismissed and took it badly (as his nature suggested he would).

Fulgentius went on reading, his vision clouded by indignation: it was a breach of trust for that man to be treating his wife as the wronged party. Claudius stressed that she had to bear the full burden of caring for the child, since the parents were otherwise occupied: the mother, a substitute vestal at the temple of Neptune, was on duty because some statues were being inaugurated, and the father, director of a gladiatorial academy, had to supervise examinations on that day. The other grandparents couldn't be asked to lend a hand: they were too preoccupied with their divorce. Which left the Legate's wife, who had to drop whatever she was doing, get to her daughter's new place in Hazel Grove, and spend all day looking after the little devil. The impertinent administrator had the nerve to find it unfair that the worthy matron, at her age, after all she had done for her own children, should be left with the heavy lifting and the consequent cost to her body, a body, he added, that in spite of the years, still displayed the nobility of its lineage ... And he went on like that, completely out of line. Had he forgotten that he was writing to her husband? No, he hadn't, because the real message was there to read between the lines: she was holding the domestic fort, coping with everything that came up, while he was on tour, free as a bird, playing at war ...

It was outrageous that an employee should reproach him in that way, but what he really couldn't get over was the utter absurdity of it all. The message had crossed rivers, mountains, and deserts, taking three months to arrive and inform him of something as transient as the cough of a child in rude health, who had no doubt recovered the following day. What was he supposed to do? Turn the legion around and show up in Rome three months later to ask about a cough that no one would remember, from half a year ago? It was laughable, really, but Fulgentius couldn't help being overcome by irritation.

He preserved a certain inner equanimity nevertheless, and the fit of pique did at least serve to conjure up a vision of the eternal battle between Reason and Unreason. Fulgentius served the former and the constant attacks of the latter had, so far, met with his determined resistance. But would it always be that way? He sometimes felt that it was him against the world. And he was well aware that the other side had powerful siren songs at its disposal. The idea of cheerfully throwing logic overboard and behaving like a lunatic was not without charm; it would be like leaving your luggage behind and setting off to explore the world, light as air, astride the iridescent pony of stupidity. But it was not for him; he had not been born to throw anything overboard. Still, he could add the irrational to reason, like a sculptor who finds, on finishing his Venus, that there is some marble left over and so as not to waste it endows the goddess with a third foot, growing out of her neck.

The incident was soon forgotten. It was buried by new events, and new decisions that had to be carefully considered, such as ordering the legionaries to tie back their hair. Long hair had been in fashion for some years, but Fulgentius had observed that it tended to get in the soldiers' eyes when they were fighting, and although they swore that it didn't bother them, it could obscure their vision at a crucial moment. They were too disciplined to ignore an order but they also found ingenious ways to bend the rules. So the most elaborate buns and braids began to appear on their heads, growing ever more complex and architectonic as the stylists rivaled one another. The time they spent on those constructions was taken away from the maintenance of their kit, so they had to be called to order once again. Although they had entered a peaceful zone, skirmishes could not be ruled out, and getting their helmets on would be a problem.

The peace was prolonged by a meeting that Fulgentius had keenly anticipated. According to his local informants, the legion was about to enter the territories acquired by the Countess Orsini. It was rumored that this enterprising aristocrat had created a miniature kingdom sheltered from political strife and defended by a private army, where she lived in luxury and repose. Everybody wanted to know how she had managed to do this, but thanks to the kingdom's remoteness and strictly guarded privacy the case was still cloaked in the mists of legend. The Legate did not want to miss this opportunity to see for himself what truth there might be to the rumors.

There was a preliminary contact: the legion received emissaries, who met with the plenum of centurions and began by announcing that their mistress was opposed to any kind of separate peace. This was enough to create a positive impression, as separate peace treaties had always been a headache for the empire. There followed an invitation to visit the countess.

The legion set off. They were three hours' march away. The

lady clearly had a good eye for a site: blue mountains, fragrant woods, lakes, yellow clover. Night began to fall, and the sky took on superficial violet hues, edged with gold. Birds and frogs were singing. Bees buzzed; the air drew near and then withdrew; the men began to talk to themselves.

When they reached the foot of a mountain, the guides pointed to a vast white construction clinging to the slope, three quarters of the way up. Fulgentius suggested that the legionaries could camp on the plain, but was told that they were all included in the invitation. He pointed out that the legion was six thousand strong, but the guides brushed his warning aside with a smirk: there was plenty of room for them all, as long as a few didn't mind sharing the caldarium. This convinced the soldiers that they were soon to be welcomed in conditions of unrivaled magnificence. And when they arrived, they saw that their expectations had fallen short. The three days they spent in the complex, although not sufficient to spoil them completely, provided a comprehensive introduction to the lifestyle of the rich. Hours went by as they lolled in the aromatic baths or drank by pools roiling with rare carp or tasted the dishes on constant offer. The gardens scattered among the buildings, the terraces with vast outlooks, the songs of the birds, and the colors of the flowers competed with the sensuality of hundreds of obliging slaves.

Fulgentius tried not to seem intimidated. He had known rich people, in fact he had always moved in wealthy circles, but this was a whole new dimension. The countess herself appeared to be a perfectly ordinary woman. She did not wear jewelry or fancy clothes. Although she was warm and attentive to her visitor, he did not see much of her. Having checked that he had everything he needed, she said that she was going to have a manicure, and disappeared for the rest of the morning. She was middle-aged, still attractive, and always surrounded by a cloud of assistants. There must have been meetings and negotiations under way all the time in that giant labyrinth. In one of their chats, she told Fulgentius that this was her getaway house: here she reconnected with her playful side and left her duties behind; all she did was discuss new plants with the gardeners or have the statues rearranged or converse with her guests. But before she could finish painting this Edenic picture, she was called away and excused herself with a smile ... From the little that Fulgentius was able to glean about the activities of the countess, she had various other residences in the major Pannonian cities, from which she presided over a financial network with interests in farming and mining. However much she boasted about her splendid leisure, business pursued her and she did not flee it.

Fulgentius found himself amply supplied with pleasures and amusements: they sprang forth before him at every step he took in the complex. From the private caldarium and frigidarium in his rooms he walked out onto his own terrace wearing a seamless tunic, and was served by silent slaves. In the gardens he inspected the rows of marble and bronze monsters, the various roses, the columns and paths. His legionaries, lodged in the upper bedrooms and no doubt influenced by their surroundings, behaved like gentlemen.

The thought of living in such luxury was seductive, but what would it cost? To make enough money you would have to work seriously, not just for a couple of weeks but a whole lifetime. And even if you inherited a ready-made fortune, you would still have to take care of the goods and chattels, the properties, and the staff ... It was better to visit that world for a few days and then return to reality. That way you could appreciate it better. Because if you lived there permanently, it would end up seeming normal.

The visit also allowed Fulgentius to take a broader view of his life than he could in the midst of his day-to-day bustle and see it from the other side of the contrast. He had done nothing to accumulate material wealth. Unconsciously falling in with the opinions of others, he had always put this down to laziness or incapacity or the fact that his professional and family duties had left him no time to think ahead and mount longer-term projects. Now suddenly he saw his life as one long spiritual quest, in which war had served as a form of ascesis. Barely out of childhood, he had taken up the spear and the shield, and they had conditioned his humanity. In the service of the empire, he had traveled the world and surveyed all the ways of being a man. And he had chosen this way, the flame with which Roman honor lit the fire of identity. As the impulsive wild boar pursues his mate in the dim light of winter, driven by the sovereign reproductive instinct, so had he pursued the

ideal of the centurion, in whose image he had sought to repro-
duce transient Civilization. His work consisted of the forests
and the rivers, the lands whose gods had yielded to the legions,
the skies that had reddened as the eagles took flight. Thanks to
the countless variations of war, he had remained unchanged,
master of his acts and words. Master of his death as well, which
he kept safe in his heart, as the only value for which he could
exchange all the rest.

WITH THE ONSET OF WINTER, MILITARY OPERATIONS were suspended. The legion prepared itself for a long recess, which was to take place in a pleasant corner of Cernonium, as the general staff had planned, following the advice of informants familiar with the region. There they were greeted by the first snows: tentative flurries of cottony flakes resisting gravity. They pitched their tents in rows that followed the contours of the terrain, driving the stakes deep into the earth, which would not freeze for some time yet. When it did, the tents would be stubbornly anchored until the spring thaw. This would secure them against winds and storms but also against premature marching orders, whether issued on a whim or for urgent reasons. The tents were as firmly planted as trees. The men celebrated by taking naps.

The still waters of a blue lake stretched away from the foot of the camp. Mountains, clouds, and forests of towering trees composed the landscape. Squadrons of birds crossing the sky as they migrated south announced the coming of the cold. Other birds remained, and could be heard calling from the woods. A centuries-old silence filled the surrounding space, broken by the shouts and laughter of children from neighboring villages. Curiosity overcame their fear of the giants from Rome. It was a region of goatherds and carters, prospering in their primitive way, to judge from their chubby and warmly clad offspring. While the legion was busy setting up camp, contact with the locals was delayed, but it would be frequent in the following months.

The days shrank swiftly. The night grew like a well-nourished baby whale. The soldiers knew that very soon there would scarcely be time to get anything done, so they made the best of the dwindling light, redirecting the impetus that had brought them all that way, scouting and getting to know the surrounding area. There were excursions, climbs, and hunts, which became less energetic and frequent as the days grew shorter, until eventually the men were overtaken by a great laziness. The tension slackened; yawns marked the coming of winter as accurately as the ants sealing up their nests, and the dying of the flies. The hardened warriors grew soft in their plush bearskins; their eyes closed, their breathing evened out. In the third week the lake froze over. The men burst their chrysalids in a fit of playfulness, and took up skating. In mobs of a hundred, they wheeled around on the thick crystalline layer, tracing endless circuits, smiling intently as they surrendered to the glide, oblivious to all the rest as if they were solving mathematical problems. The snow dust that had built up on the surface of the lake flew off to each side of the passing blades, forming ephemeral wings reminiscent of Mercury's sandals.

The camp sank into sleep. Behind the men's closed eyelids, all that they had experienced on the journey returned as a series of transparent images, back to the day before their departure, which reappeared in transfigured form: a soft Coliseum swaying in the air of an inexistent dawn, sirens in a hippodrome, even the baths of Caracalla inflating and deflating; movement forgotten in a motionless fall. The snow began to pile up on the earth; each morning its volumes were different, like memories. A sleepless soldier said he had seen it writhing around like a pack of animals, but nobody believed him. Dreams were spilling over into reality.

This state of things did not last. Following the example of the children, the local villagers overcame their timidity and began to visit. The population of Cernonium was divided into separate groups, living in territories delimited by custom and by the torrents flowing down from the Carpathians. The region had become a trade corridor linking the two Pannonias, and oxen were bred there to draw carts loaded with bronze for statuary. Careful crossbreeding over centuries had produced animals of colossal dimensions. And it was with a team of such brutes as a welcoming gift that a representative delegation of Cernonians came to visit. General Fulgentius received them with stern courtesy, in full dress uniform, and engaged them in conversation. But if he supposed that he had thereby fulfilled the demands of etiquette, he was mistaken. The divisions within the population conspired against his peace of mind. Another delegation presented itself the following day, unaware of the first. And then another, and yet another ... Each requested an audience, apologizing profusely: they didn't want to cause any inconvenience; they were happy to meet wherever and whenever he chose. Even so, they made their requests, and insinuated that it would be mean-spirited of him to decline, since he had nothing else to do, which was more or less the case, but they had no right to make that presumption. He realized that their motive was mere curiosity, which was understandable, since they were unlikely to get another chance to see a real Roman general. He was flattered, but that didn't make up for the inconvenience. He had to get dressed and wait (they were not models of punctuality), and listen to them for hours, because although they came with the declared intention of hearing about his exploits as the legion's commander, as soon as they arrived, they started talking about their own affairs, as if he cared. It was torture. He would get up in the morning thinking about the people he had to meet and greet, and the wasted afternoon ahead, and a hopeless feeling would come over him.

"Why don't you say no?" asked Lactarius, tired of hearing him complain.

"Do you think I could afford to do that?" Hope rang in his voice like an avid chime.

"The general in command of the Lupine Legion can afford to do almost anything, your Excellency. Perhaps it's what they're expecting you to do. They probably think you'd be offended if they didn't ask for an audience. It might be as much of a bother for them."

Fulgentius needed no further encouragement. He declined the next request, referring to urgent obligations, used the same excuse from then on, and freed himself of the visitors. He supposed that he would get a reputation for being unapproachable, but he liked the thought of inspiring legends about the inaccessible general, absorbed in tasks so secret that they would come to seem prodigious. Sometimes remaining hidden is more conducive to fame—especially the sort of fame worth having—than putting oneself on display.

With time on his hands, Fulgentius got to thinking, and went over the ups and downs of the journey, which formed a mobile mosaic of colors and shapes in his memory. Having put this picture in some kind of order, he noticed a discrepancy between what had actually happened and the plan that he had made before setting out. No surprise there: it was always like that. The facts had a thousand ways of failing to meet expectations, as if they enjoyed being different. And it was just as well, because the mind's mistakes about reality were the best antidote to boredom.

But the discrepancy in this case gave him food for thought. The plan had been to skip from city to city, from one performance of his play to the next. A neat chain of productions, each standing out against a background of sameness, the marches between them dotted here and there with brisk massacres; all this without compromising his official mission, since his eagerness to reach the next stopping place (and performance) would impart an urgency to the military tasks. Of course it had not turned out like that. Although he had thought that his tragedy was the only thing that mattered to him, he had been distracted by other events and characters. He wondered whether in making his plan he might have been influenced by the structure of literary works, with their cantos or chapters of similar length, each containing an episode. Real life didn't unfold with that sort of regular rhythm. The brief and the lasting were all mixed up; long spans of time were full of brevities, and brevity itself often harbored interminable durations.

This train of thought led him back to his tragedy. He felt the creative itch again, and wondered why he had gone for months without seeing his work performed, simply because he hadn't been in a city with a theater company. Where was his initiative? The inventiveness that had once moved him to write should have risen to the challenge. Toying with the idea of putting on a production right there and directing it himself, Fulgentius glimpsed a dimension of theater that was new to him: the real work that made it truly theatrical, work that struck him as akin to that of a sculptor or interior decorator. He had seen his play produced often enough to deduce the steps required to achieve the final result. Directing would be a new experience. It was exciting because it would bring him into more intimate contact with his play, as if he were literally handling its material, which is to say, the text.

Fulgentius was so taken with the idea that he was in no hurry to put it into practice. He wanted to savor it in imagination. Since he had mentioned his plan to no one but Lactarius, from whom he kept no secrets, the change that occurred in his behavior over the following days remained inexplicable to the men and began to attract attention. Or perhaps it was explicable but in a disturbing way. The general took to walking slowly around the camp, up and down the rows of tents. He had never done such a thing before. He was, in fact, thinking about the cast, which he would select from the legionaries. He believed that choosing the right actor for each role was more important than directing. Finding someone who looked the part was half the work; more than half—almost all of it. With the play's characters in his head, he went prospecting. And with six thousand idle men at his disposal, he was spoiled for choice. He took his time, observing them at leisure, searching for the perfect match. He had never examined his men like that before.

And they had never been examined in that way. Preoccupied by his search, Fulgentius was blind to the unease that he caused by stopping in front of a legionary and running his eye over the man's entire anatomy. Since no one knew what he was up to, the conjectures multiplied, all based on the supposition that his motive was carnal pleasure. That look meant one thing and one thing only. And they could hardly say no to the general. They were puzzled. To the query, "Isn't he married?" came the classic riposte: "They're the worst." Not that hardened legionaries on active service were afraid of sodomy; but the deep indecision suggested by the general's repeated staring provoked new anxieties.

When Lactarius came to hear of the rumor—nothing could escape his notice for long—he informed his master, who gave himself the classic slap on the forehead, exclaiming: "How stupid of me!" He blamed himself for being thoughtless, but not for too long; after all, the men were to blame for jumping to conclusions. And he was surprised by their prudishness.

The misunderstanding was cleared up, the cast was duly chosen, and anticipation began to build, although Fulgentius warned that he would be taking his time. He handed out the scrolls so that the actors could learn their parts, but for the time being he put off the start of rehearsals. There was no hurry. Winter had barely begun. And he didn't want to infect his theatrical work with the noise and vulgarity of the Saturnalia, so he would have to wait until the festivities were over. Waiting was not a problem, once the men had worked the military tensions out of their systems. They had nothing to do but there were plenty of distractions. Beggars, mystics, and peddlers visited: a dormant legion was a powerful magnet for curiosity and opportunism. Nubile young women came fishing, sassy and prissy by turns. Gray squirrels descended from the mountains and were killed for their skins, which were used to make warm gloves. The little foxes had better luck; the men adopted them as pets and even tried, without success, to train them. Fulgentius reconnoitered the surrounding area. Having heard of some abandoned cities, he set out to visit them, but was unable to explore the ruins of the ancient temples because they were full of snakes, active in spite of the winter cold, like the rabbits on which they preyed.

Proud lords of the forest, the wolves had followed the legion and settled near the camp. They assumed their role as totems of the empire's most famous military machine, sharing its invincibility. The plump and sleepy females awaited the first stirrings of spring, when they would whelp. The males moved across the wooded slopes, breaking the crust of the snow. They had won the legionaries' respect, in so far as the incarnation of a symbol can be respected by humans.

This entente came to an end in one of those moments of heightened clarity immediately following a snowfall. The king of the wolves, the pack's dominant male, was sitting, as usual, on a high rock, from which he could survey the whole camp. He seemed to be consciously exhibiting his emblematic status. He knew (as animals know these things) that he was admired, almost venerated. And he was perfectly silhouetted against the brightness of the sky. It was too much of a temptation for the archer who slept in every legionary. One of them yielded. An arrow went flying and pierced the wolf's heart. The archer was applauded, as was the man who roasted the animal's succulent loin over the coals that night. They had never eaten wolf flesh before but perhaps this was the beginning of a tradition for the Lupine Legion. After all, eating totemic animals was a custom that dated back to primitive times, those hallowed days of old.

This reasoning moderated the anger that rose in Fulgentius when he found out. The whole heroico-poetic fiction that he had crafted around the compatibility between wolf and legion was falling apart because of the silliness and brutality of his men. Once moderated, his anger gave way to approval. He had always been opposed to mysticism and legends. The wolf was just another furry beast, and the totem story was better left to Ovid.

Finally he decided to begin rehearsals. He had delayed so long that the members of the cast had learned their parts down to the last word. They had taken it seriously, it seemed. And they must have been rehearsing amongst themselves in secret because the dialogues flowed smoothly right from the start. As soon as they were put in place, they rattled off their lines like parrots. Fulgentius was slightly disappointed; they were making it too easy for him. He had imagined that he would be doing something more creative than simply telling them to start and watching how they did it. He was bored. Could it have been the play that was boring him, the play that had charmed and moved him for years? He wondered if "handling the material" of his tragedy might render it inoperative, like a broken toy. He even considered abandoning the project.

He would have done so if not for an accident, which changed his mind. He had put off casting the only female part: that of the princess, whose intervention triggers the hero's ultimate demise. It was pointed out to him that there were long scenes, crucial to the plot's unfolding, that could not be rehearsed without her.

"But who could play the role?"

The question spread through the legion like spilled oil, iridescent and sticky. To the general's dumbfounded surprise, about a hundred men volunteered. He couldn't believe it. Veteran centurions, survivors of a thousand battles, shaggy legionaries hardened by campaigns throughout the cisalpine lands, brooding Sicilians, Neapolitans with curly beards (which they offered to shave off), he-men visibly rippling with muscle, all competing to put on the silks and mincing ways of a dubious virgin. "Hang on," Fulgentius thought. "Weren't you all scandalized when you thought I was looking for a lover?"

In the end, Fulgentius chose a woman—one of the slaves the countess had offered him as a parting gift—more to teach his men a lesson than because he thought she would do the best job. She was young, her body was superb, and she had the typically vacant features of Sarmatian beauties, who always seemed to be thinking of something else. The aspirants were noisy in their complaints but the general stood his ground. They said the girl didn't speak Latin and wouldn't be able to learn her speeches. She didn't even know what theatre was; she wouldn't understand his instructions. "You'll have to manipulate her as if she were a wooden doll," they said. And he replied: "So what?"

Their objections inspired Fulgentius to breathe new life into a dramatic project that had seemed moribund. He realized that until then, he had been thinking of a conventional production, like all the others he had seen. But there was no reason why he should do what everybody else did. No one was forcing him; on the contrary. He had decided to direct the play himself precisely in order to go his own way, and that opened up a range of possibilities. The princess, for example, could be a purely decorative presence; she didn't have to understand what was being said or why she was there or what was going on ... It would make the plot more ambiguous and mysterious. Having realized that this was only one of the transgressive innovations with which he might enrich the play, he recovered his enthusiasm, and the rehearsals went ahead.

Although nothing was happening—that was the whole idea
of winter quarters—things were happening all the time. One
of them affected the general personally. As always, the legion
attracted locals like a magnet: peddlers of handicrafts and local
delicacies, musicians, holy men, or simply busybodies. Not a
few young men came to offer themselves as recruits. They were
automatically turned away; the soldiers didn't even bother to
explain that the Lupine Legion was an elite corps, drawn from
the best of the imperial militias; it had no time to train novices.
There were female camp followers too. Sexual mores were re-
markably relaxed in Pannonia. Young women, pretty in their
exotic way, came like fawns to a spring, and gave themselves
with grateful smiles to the burly legionaries. The men, long
tried by the hysterical demands of Roman women, gave themselves in turn, as if in an Edenic adolescence.

One of those who found pleasure in the arms of a beautiful young Pannonian was Lactarius. As the weeks went by, his
infatuation intensified. The couple went from kissing and cud-
dling in the woods to passionate embraces in the tent when
Fulgentius was out at rehearsals. The girl returned to her home
in the village at night, where her parents, she said, kept close
watch over her. This did not displease her lover, as it gave the
romance an atmosphere of furtive provisionality. The short
days made their time together more precious, as with any other
scarce good. One day the girl lingered beyond sundown, explaining that her parents had gone to the mountains for a sha-
manic retreat. Lactarius invited her to dinner in the officers'
mess, after which they went for a walk under the stars, and the

young man, burning with desire by this point, saw an opportunity to make love in the tent, by the firelight, which would coat their bodies with golden surfaces of pleasure. The problem was that it all depended on the approval and complicity of Fulgentius, who had already gone to bed. Lactarius was in a quandary. He had boasted to the girl that he was the general's favorite.

"I don't think his favors will stretch to going out and leaving us alone in the tent, on a night as cold as this," she said.

"I never ask him for anything. Just this once, he could indulge me."

"What if he proposes a threesome? That would be really awkward."

"He'd never do that!" exclaimed Lactarius, deeply shaken in his loyalty, and slightly taken aback by his girlfriend's imagination. "General Fulgentius is the most decent man in the world."

In the end, he fell back on the trusty formula "no harm in trying," and decided to ask. Fulgentius was lying down but not asleep, reading by the light of an oil lamp. He responded favorably to the request, almost to the point of thanking his assistant. He found those endless nights so boring; he was glad of an excuse to get up and go out. He wrapped himself in a bearskin and went to wake the slave boy.

"The kid can stay," said Lactarius. "He sleeps so deeply, all Hannibal's elephants marching past and shaking the earth wouldn't wake him up. My athletics with Alba will be far less noisy."

"No. I'll take him with me. There are times when I can't do without him."

Fulgentius woke the slave boy with difficulty or at least got him to walk in his sleep, and they went out, leaving the bed free for the lovers. The general and the boy walked down to the shore of the lake to contemplate that celestial prodigy, the moon, shining on the ice and snow of the mountains, which sparkled against the black backdrop of the night. The boy fell asleep again, curled up at the general's feet. Fulgentius stood there thinking and dreaming. His gaze slid over the smooth, clean surface of the frozen lake. The men had cut holes in it to fish, but they never caught anything. At that time of night and in that state of mind, it might all have been a dream. The men's persistence in dropping a hook through a hole in the ice and waiting for hours, even when experience had proved the futility of the endeavor, was so absurd as not to seem entirely real. And that was not the only thing at odds with the laws of reality. But if it was a dream, no one but he could have been the dreamer. The last thing he remembered was the fish that wouldn't nibble at the bottom of the lake, and this was the key to all his earlier memories. The moon continued to climb in the sky, where autobiographical solitude, the mother of all melancholy, was taking up residence.

The vigil gave him ideas. He found everything inspiring— whatever happened, whatever he saw—no doubt because he was in a state of theatrical activity, which was a state of natural and continuous inspiration. Nothing was lost, nothing was useless, since everything could pass into art. In everyday life many things were lost and almost everything was useless, but thanks to the discreet miracle of art, all was pure gain. In this case it was a matter of perfecting a feature of the performance that he had already begun to develop: he liked the way the princess took part in the play without saying a word or knowing what theatre was. In order to maximize the effect, he decided that she would remain on stage the whole time: an intruder, an inexplicable presence. She would, of course, be there in the scenes involving her character but since she would never reply, the speeches addressed to her would fall flat. He put this idea into practice the following day and found it perversely enjoyable. In that he was alone. The actors complained: if the princess was speechless, the action was incomprehensible. He told them to be quiet. He wasn't going to have them getting uppity about meaning. He was the only one who had any business grasping it or not.

It wasn't quite true, however, that he could use anything at all to enrich the play with formal details. He had noticed something rather paradoxical. The most trivial and insignificant things (a breath of wind, a shadow, a crumb in the beard of a soldier) were the most productive. By contrast, the most spectacular and memorable events turned out to be unusable. This was confirmed by the visit of a man for whom he broke his resolution not to receive any more strangers. Fulgentius was not the only one to drop everything and yield to curiosity, with good reason. The visitor was a fat Armenian with a mustache, decked with jewels, leading a train of a hundred camels. The animals, accustomed to a different climate, were numb with cold. The Armenian's assistants brushed the melting snow off their humps, and threw bright blankets over their backs or tied them around their heads like turbans. The sight of those creatures, with their sad saggy lips and expressive eyes, could not have been more grotesque. Having admired the train, Fulgentius invited the Armenian to his tent. The man was heading for Rome to sell the beasts.

"Is there a market for so many?"

"The buyers will be fighting over them, even if I set a high price and raise it as they sell. The last one will go for a fortune."

"But what do they want them for? Other animals are more practical for carrying and hauling, not to mention riding."

The Armenian chuckled knowingly.

"My dear general, I fear that as a Roman you may not be ideally placed to comprehend the tendencies of the society to which you belong. You live within them, and they can only be seen from the outside."

"And what is to be seen from that privileged point of view? Please do enlighten me."

"Without going into details or retracing the history that led up to this point, I can tell you that many of your compatriots, between the Capitoline and Aventine Hills, are prepared to pay the price of ten Nubian slaves for a camel to decorate the garden."

A whistle of astonishment issued from the lips of Fulgentius. He changed the subject:

"I have been told that the natural beauty of your land is beyond compare."

"Do you mean Armenia? Not that I've noticed, although my

business has taken me from one end of the country to the other. What are you referring to exactly?"

"I have heard descriptions of green mountains, blue valleys, transparent lakes, paths that wind among the clouds ..."

"Oh, all that. I wouldn't recommend it. The place is full of robbers."

"But exactly. That must complete the panorama and make it even more interesting: seeing those men from afar, in the gigantic mountain passes, tiny as insects; the vastness would seem vaster still, more majestic ... And the colors of the mountains, softened by the transient mists and, beyond, the silhouettes of other ranges, which might turn out to be clouds ..."

He didn't pursue this evocation. There was no point: the Armenian wasn't listening. Aesthetic sensibility was unevenly distributed. All that coarse-minded merchant could see in the wonders of nature was the risk of being robbed of one of his stupid camels.

As it was late in the afternoon, Fulgentius invited the Armenian to spend the night in the camp; that would give the general time to write a letter to his wife, which the merchant kindly offered to deliver. He moved the camels away because, as he said, they were very noisy, and he didn't want to disturb the sleep of the legionaries. They could be heard even at a distance, and Fulgentius had to write his letter to their accompaniment.

My dear Nemesis,
  I am in good health, as I hope are all of you at home. The

campaign is proceeding as planned, without any casualties worth mentioning. The men are well nourished; the chain of command has lost no links, and the climate is as favorable as one might reasonably expect. For my part, I am discharging my duty as a soldier and a Roman. We are spending the winter in Cernonium, and although the season is not yet half over, I am already bored. I spend my time solving the major and minor problems that arise in a stationed legion, watching the snow fall, and thinking. This enforced leisure is bound to provoke reflection since there is nothing else to do. The turmoil of military life in the service of the empire affords few opportunities to stop and think about anything beyond the immediate and the urgent. When such an opportunity does arise, thought plays *fortissimo*, which is what I am experiencing now. My whole life is passing before my mind's eye, with its sorrows and its joys. I go back to the moment when we first met, no further; before that, there was only natural growth, no different from the maturation of a plant or a cat. My real life began when our hearts and lives were joined, and it has given me no cause for discontent. Our union, our wonderful children and grandchildren (by the way, I hope the little one's cough has cleared up). My professional life has been equally satisfactory: a steady climb from office to office, victories in a hundred campaigns, with the added benefit of allowing me to see the world. Few have been so lucky. To complain would be shameful, far be it from me. Why then do I feel dissatisfied and constantly strive to justify myself in my own eyes? Why this vague feeling that I have failed? Am I not being unfair to myself and those around me and above all to those who are truly suffering? It is true that this melancholy introspection reveals a delicate, somewhat feminine sensibility, but I reveal it only here in this letter, for nobody's eyes but yours. Outwardly I remain the admired and feared commander of the mighty Lupine Legion, not a crack in my façade. And yet when I commune with myself, I am battered by the swell of the void, the anguish of having lived in vain. I'm not expressing myself well but I don't know if there's a better way. The cause of the anguish is simply having lived, not having lived well or badly. That's it. I lived. That's what I regret. But there was nothing else I could do. If there were other lives, none of them was mine.

Enough of this; don't worry about me. It must be age, which holds us up with its endless preambles. What was once impatience turns into melancholy. But melancholy doesn't come unbidden, we seek it out, and there must be a reason why. Perhaps it is the only state in which thoughts can be taken to their logical conclusions, without being interrupted by the urgent demands of action. I should temper this amateur philosophizing: I don't want to sound like an old man sitting in the atrium of his house, resentfully watching the young go by. I am toiling on, and hope is the only metal to work, the only marble to sculpt. Hope or Pannonia? Perhaps I'm confusing the two. I realize that in this letter I should have been giving you an account of my journey through these regions bathed in the light of barbaric suns, with descriptions of panoramas, flowers, and birds, instead of which I have wasted time describing my dark inner states. Perhaps I could say that the letter is like my life: it should have been different but it was destined from the start to turn out as it did. I ought to begin again, keeping the few felicitous sentences, building them into a new context. I'm not happy with the result but that is nothing new. Ultimately, I think, the dissatisfaction springs from the need to occupy time, which is an impossible task because time, by definition, is the voiding of itself.

Your husband who misses you,

F.

The following day he felt as if he were emerging from a dream. He couldn't believe he had written that letter. He felt a satisfaction that his body could barely contain. Alert in all his faculties, he wondered if the key to feeling truly satisfied might be to express one's dissatisfaction so eloquently as to convince other people. Or perhaps he had bought his satisfaction cheaply, starting from a very low base level; having accomplished the tiny feat of writing a letter to his wife, he felt as if he had carried off a major victory. In any case, the dreamlike feeling persisted. He went for a walk in a daze, without realizing that the day had barely dawned. What's wrong? asked the few legionaries who were up and about, knowing how regular he was in his habits. The snowdrifts were solidifying in the light; the black pines stood guard on the mountainsides. The deep canyons echoed with the noises of the camels, far off already on their way to Rome, despite the early hour. The general felt like rereading his letter but he hadn't made a copy. That duty usually fell to Lactarius, who was temporarily indisposed, lost in the meanders of his romance. Fulgentius tried to piece the missive together in his memory but he couldn't recover much of it; no sooner had the quill inscribed his signature than he had fallen asleep.

When the high mental tension of composing was released, it propelled him into another dimension, and sleep carried off a large portion of the text. He felt as if he had used a cipher, a secret code. He had to admit that letter writing was not his forte; it was something he hardly ever did, and given the strange effect of this latest effort, he was in no hurry to do it again.

It took him some time to recover his peace of mind. The legionaries had rustled a camel from the Armenian; after his departure they brought it out of hiding and spent several days playing with it, riding it, laughing like children. There would have been no harm in this, except that the noisy animal made it hard to sleep, by day or by night. The phase of hibernation seemed to have come to an end. The men were waking up too early. To burn off the energy that had built up while they rested, they took up fencing. Reviving an exercise from their training days, they practiced with heavy swords made of stone, so that their usual iron swords would feel light by contrast. This was just a game: playing at beginners to enjoy a vicarious youth. The irregular thwock-thwock sound of hundreds of stone swords striking one another filled the white air, frightened the birds, and peppered the hexameters of the tragedy, which was rehearsed each afternoon.

The actors chosen from the legion had grown accustomed to the mute and idle presence of the princess throughout the play. She had become invisible to them, as the general noticed, watching from the high stool that gave him a bird's eye view of the stage. After a surfeit of rehearsals, they rattled off their speeches in an automatic, absentminded way, paying more attention to the noises of the camel or the stone swords than to the fates of their characters. Fulgentius let them carry on; he liked that mechanical, inhuman delivery. From time to time, mainly to prolong the rehearsal, he asked them to change positions or emphasize something or pause. Listening to the lines that he too knew by heart, he drifted off into a daydream. The rehearsal was happening inside his mind.

In the end, a delegation of actors dared to raise the issue of beginning the performances. They were reaching saturation. Fulgentius had already decided that there would be no performances at all. He had been captivated by the poetry of rehearsals. Nevertheless, he relented. What was a hidden world for him was tedium for the actors. He announced that the time had come to start building the set. Although this meant extra work, because the rehearsals would continue in the meantime, the troupe was happy to take it on, partly because it was something different but above all because the director gave them free rein to show off their creativity.

The sets were built out of snow: the Roman palace in which the fictional Fulgentius discovers his betrayal at the hands of the perfidious consuls, the caves where he took refuge, the tower where the Scythian king had imprisoned his own daughter, and the Coliseum of Shadows where the Roman hero met his death. Snow, in limitless supply, was the marble and brick of these constructions. The men worked enthusiastically, building each new set over the old one, circulating among white masses that transported them to an imaginary world, and the work, that is, the rehearsal, was enriched as a result.

Fulgentius and the slave boy had grown accustomed to managing on their own since they couldn't rely on Lactarius, who had been under the spell of his girlfriend, day and night, for weeks. This situation came to a sudden end. One day they found him on his own, which in itself was unusual, and in tears. He tried to hide it but his heart was overflowing. The girl had broken off their relationship. After some days of silence and dodging the issue, she had finally apprised him of her decision, which was final and of a piece with her earlier choice to give herself freely, outright, and ask for nothing in return. She had sweetened the pill by telling him that they would go on being friends, that her affection for him remained, that they would always have the memory of those beautiful moments but ...

"But what?"

Here the general's young assistant, pouring out his sorrow, sobbingly repeated her predictable reasons for breaking it off: their relationship had no future; he had his career in the legion all mapped out while she still had to make her way, and to do that, she had to be free to meet young men from her own world, to fall in love, get married, and start a family.

"Where did she get the idea that my career was mapped out? I'm just an assistant, more junior than the most junior decurion ... And I'm two years younger than she is!"

Fulgentius abstained from reminding Lactarius of the way he must have boasted about his position on the general's staff.

He thought it better to console his assistant with words that a father might have used.

"My dear Lactarius, I didn't think you were so naive or so little versed in the ways of the world. These winter romances should be treated as such, enjoyed while they last, and brought to a timely end."

"But the bitch could have waited till spring! What difference would it have made to her?"

"It's better this way. You've been spared my disapproval, which would have coincided with nature's cruel renewal of the life cycle: the terrible green that returns to remind us we have to go through it all over again. If your girlfriend hadn't been in a hurry to give you a kick in the butt, the bad news would have come all at once. This way you'll have had time to get over the dumping and gather your strength to face the wretchedness of spring."

To cheer Lactarius up, Fulgentius gave him a brightly colored sled and took him to see the snow palaces built by the actors. The young man gazed in awe. How much he had missed by falling in love! But he would be present for the best, which was yet to come. In the heart of winter, the great storms erupted, with winds so strong it seemed they would tear the mountains up by their roots. The tents held firm, and the men resigned themselves to staying in and playing dice or sleeping. The props and sets made of snow, however, were twisted by the wind into oyster-like shapes, which were greatly admired. Chance directed by the forces of nature was a divine artist, whose whims had to be indulged. The young slave who played the princess rashly ventured out in the middle of a storm, was seized by a whirlwind, flung a mile through the air, and dashed against the rock face of a mountain. She was the only casualty, just as she had been the only woman in the cast. When the clouds withdrew the nights were lit by the dance of the stars, and the men went out riding. Then the weather got bad again; the snow froze hard as stone, and sleep returned. These and other alternations occupied the remainder of their sojourn.

WITH THE FIRST SIGNS OF THE COMING WARMTH, THE legion opened like a flower, a great iron flower from which the returning sun struck blinding flashes. The mass of soldiers formed the corolla: the infantrymen were the petals, the horsemen the sepals, the decurions the stamens, and the centurions the carpels. The huge metallic-blue monocotyledon lit up like a trumpet blown by Boreas. The flower's volume, determining its form and function, was constituted by the courage of the men, the oath they had taken to lay down their lives for the Capitol. The pistil, swathed in iridescent dust, with a droplet of fragrant syrup on its tip, was the Unknown Centurion, to whom prayers were offered up, as to an equestrian household god. The calyx, coated with costly platinum, slowly spread its lamellae to reveal the white pollen that nourishes dreams. If spring had come as an anticlimax, like all past and future springs, with the same trees and birds, and the same sense of futility burdening the heart, if the men shackled themselves reluctantly to the present, the opening of the great flower was a reminder that within each one of them ten thousand flowers were opening. the ardors of martial sanctity. Fertilization was beginning. The bumblebee that had eaten the atom took flight.

The lake thawed from one day to the next. Crazy with joy,

out of control, the fish raced each other, and rose to the surface
to look at the air with eyes like jade sesterces. Their exuberance
stirred up whirlpools and rocked the remaining chunks of ice,
which knocked white chips off each other. Everything was waking up. The jubilant whistling of the marmots betrayed the lo-
cation of the mountains: stone giants clothed in nightgowns of
mist, still asleep, taking their first uncertain steps. Flies sprang
from the earth; the ducks returned; from the woods came roars
and trills. Immaculate clouds hurried past overhead. What had
been snow-filled gorges were once again torrents where the
tadpole and the bubble reigned. Hungry birds gave their bills
no rest. Tree-dwelling roosters crowed on branches, ruffling
their yellow plumage, sporting crimson combs. Unruly fauna
made a racket day and night. Calling to each other with elytra
and scents, keeping appointments made in other summers, the
animals found each other like symmetries. If any went without
a mate, it was by choice.

The legionaries dismantled the camp and loaded the wag-
ons, taking charge of a reality that had been buried in snow.
Before setting off there was a session of collective hairdress-
ing, to tidy the men up and make them presentable. During
the months of hibernation they had let their hair grow wild,
along with their beards and nails, like cave men. They shook off
the last residues of sleep, warily contemplating the near future.
They threw off shells of liquid crystal, discovering their old
muscles formed anew, the silver cartilage forged by the storms.
They had learned how to sleep but what use was that now they

had woken? They were waiting like children to be told what to do. The hair cut off lay on the ground, in the puddles of snow-melt. The sleds, the bones, and the heavy furs were abandoned: the debris of a picnic for six thousand guests. The legionaries left everything in a mess, accustomed as they were to having their dirty work done by others; they were busy enough with the Senate's dirty work.

After a few days' marching they had left immobility behind. They were recovering the use of their joints, breathing new at-mospheres. They were going where they were told to go, like obedient children who also happened to be titans of ferocity. In his cocoon, Fulgentius felt fragile. The tasks that lay ahead, he knew, were much more arduous than any he had carried out so far. He had known this when he accepted the command of the mission: when they reached the heart of Pannonia, they would have to eliminate the insurgency that had militarized what should have been a hub of peaceful production. That meant war, battles, nights on alert: a bloodier, more deplorable waste of time than anything in Hades. Once they crossed the black mountains, the timeless time of winter would give way to a dense succession of instants: the urgent temporal cells of war. They would have to say goodbye to thought and welcome the primitive survival reflexes. Survival had been an issue during the winter recess too but in its slow, white version. And as long as time was willing, one could always survive time.

There was no escape or hope of delay for they were already entering the heart of Pannonia. That metaphor pursued them, always triumphing over geography. They passed through various regions identified on the maps as Hyrcania, Valaquia, Carinthia, Moravia, Dalmatia ... but it was all Pannonia, and they were always entering its heart. It was futile to attribute distinctive features to these regions, for example Carinthia, where Fulgentius issued a special warning about the horned vipers, those splendid, checkered queens of the ground, with their lethal fangs, native to the territory (so he had read in Pliny). For a month they advanced as if walking on eggs but even that frightening realism had to yield to Pannonia's mobile heart, which they were always entering.

Since the trading routes that linked the Empire's eastern and western sectors had to pass through the heart of Pannonia, the Lupine Legion's key task was to clear the zone of all resistance. But the heart's supposed centrality was curiously contradicted by its strategic importance as a corridor between regions that existed in their own right. Perhaps all centers were empty, thought Fulgentius, and that was what made them centers. Even so, the mere possibility that the empty and the full might be the same was poison to his mind.

In any case the hostilities would not be long in coming. The legion marched on, keeping up its guard, with a cordon around the camp at night, roving parties ahead and behind, dissuasive noises, and plumes standing proud. There was no chance of the natural beauty distracting the soldiers to the point where they might be taken by surprise or fall into an ambush. This was obviously a good thing, but Fulgentius would have liked his men to realize just how lucky they were to have before their eyes and beneath their feet a sample of pristine Nature, still unspoiled by human activity. It could not be called totally virgin territory since it was known to hunters, shepherds, and travelers, but the flora and fauna had not suffered the depredations that inevitably follow population growth, the consequent exploitation of resources, and, with urbanization and mechanization, the loss of respect for the wilderness.

And apart from the fact that the rough legionaries had no time for such refinements, how could one appreciate the privilege of a previous state, of living before what had not yet occurred? The present was previous to the future, of course, but it wasn't all that obvious that it was a privileged point in time, especially when the *immediate* future promised the scarlet clamor of battle.

It was on the Dalmatian plains that they met with the first serious opposition. The enemy carried massive objects to hurl at the invaders. Although crude, their arms were effective. A confrontation that lasted all day produced no conclusive result. In a tent pitched hastily by moonlight, the general consulted the commanders of the various battalions involved in the incident. It turned out that half the troops had been waiting to join battle, and no one had a clear sense of what had happened, if indeed anything had. Each time the legionaries had dashed ahead, the enemy forces were conspicuously absent. They had simply failed to show. This lack of coordination drove Fulgentius to despair. He didn't know how he'd be able to sleep, with all his worries piling up, and without sleep, the following day, at the critical moments, he too would be absent, drowsy, unable to concentrate. He didn't want to resort to the experts' herbal preparations, because if he came to depend on them for getting to sleep, it would not serve him well.

Learning the art of war was like training a dog: there was a system of patiently administered rewards and punishments, which gradually established mental parameters for appropriate and inappropriate behavior. Except that a dog would learn in the end, if it wasn't too obtuse, while a soldier went on receiving rewards and punishments all his life and if he started to rely on what he had learned, he was lost.

The first setbacks necessitated a revision of the strategy. Fulgentius had too much faith in his men to be seriously worried: being human they might fail individually, but jointly they were protected by the invincible shield of the legion's prestige. They were unaffected by the sultry weather. If a fault was to be found with them, it was overconfidence. So, with a mental shrug, the general ordered them to launch flanking maneuvers, send in the cavalry, channel their inner turmoil, and crush the locals.

It was the same, mutatis mutandis, when they had to traverse the black Balkans, defended by troops that were no less lethal for being scattered and elusive. Fighting in the mountains, the legionaries had to take account of the law of gravity, which was irresistibly at work although not yet supplied with a scientific formulation. Shooting an arrow downward multiplied its velocity and force, as the ambushers, perched on porphyry ledges, were well aware, and this obliged the legionaries to hold their shields over their heads all the time, like parasols, which led to painful straining of the shoulder tendons. When the officers relayed their complaints to the general, he issued a stern reprimand. He had to remind them that the legion was not some private enterprise, in which slaves might have (or usurp) the right to demand better working conditions, which the master might be well advised to grant, in order to increase productivity. The defense of the empire was a question of life and death, not of the paltry wellbeing of slaves.

But inwardly he couldn't help agreeing with them: it was pretty pathetic shooting arrows up into the air, as if they were hunting birds. The projectile left the bow limply, half-heartedly, turned around as soon as possible, and finally picked up speed as it fell, with all the sarcasm an inanimate object can betray. The alternative was to take positions higher than the enemy's. That sounded good in theory but it wasn't feasible. The legionaries were not mountain goats adept at scaling crags; even if they had tried, they would never have been able to compete with the natives. So the enemy soldiers had to be drawn out onto the plain by burning their villages, raping their women, and crucifying their progeny on little child-size crosses. If that didn't bring them down from the mountains, it was proof of their heartlessness.

Combat became a daily routine. The legion swept all before it. From the mire of past experience, it extracted the resources it needed to annihilate the enemy methodically. Tired of dealing with repeated flare-ups, determined to stop at nothing, Fulgentius opted for a scorched-earth policy. Setting fires systematically, the Romans wiped out whole towns; caravans of refugees fled before the invincible columns, and no one could say how far this eastward sweep would reach. The invaders were not guided by a star or the continual whispering of the grasses but by the cruel sun. A large castle, the seat of old Hyrcanian kings, was demolished in an afternoon, with no regard for its historical value or possible recreational use by future generations. The next morning, when the legion set off, the men turned to look back and saw, or thought they saw, the castle resurrected in the mist.

Fulgentius reacted to the stubborn resistance of the natives with an irritated bafflement. They must have known that in the end all opposition would be futile; the power of the center was so clearly superior. Rome had history on its side, and history was inexorable. So why were these provincials persisting in a defense that was doomed to fail, at a huge cost in human lives and property? The most likely explanation was that they were clinging to patriotic sentiment, and were perhaps blinded by ignorance and fear of the new as well. They were isolated and always had been; that was why they granted an absolute value to their traditions and religions, their woods and mountains, the wretched furnishings of their coarse lives. Fulgentius came bearing a priceless gift: the chance to become a colony of the empire, and instead of giving thanks, they were pelting him with sticks and stones. If they had only been more receptive, he could have explained the advantages of belonging. Maybe they were afraid of having to pay taxes. True, the Roman eagles were strict about that, but there could be no free entry to the Pax Romana; and besides, they were already spending that much on showy and superfluous trifles.

Well, if it was steel they wanted, the legion would oblige. The mountains were cleansed with torrents of blood. And yet the eastward advance was arduous. The rebel forces gathered in retreat, and desperation fueled their fighting spirit as they saw their lands laid waste, their homes destroyed, and their families slaughtered. Their daring became suicidal, and the legionaries had to take extra precautions, killing them at a distance if possible. Had it not been so exhausting and inhuman, the spectacle of the clashes would have been something to contemplate: shouting men, flashing bronze, blaring trumpets, neighing horses. It wasn't every day you could see such a scene. And yet they were seeing it almost every day.

The contrast between the battle itself and the preceding day was a problem for Fulgentius. He knew that the first step was everything. But before taking that step, when he could see the enemy there in front of him and he had to give the order, and the uproar had to begin again, an invincible, anticipatory fatigue made it seem an impossible task. The temptation not go through with it was overwhelming. Especially since, having gone on the offensive by marching in uninvited, they still had the option of not attacking; the other side would be grateful, and the legion could take it easy. But that would just be procrastination, unless they abandoned their mission. It was like being drawn toward a void. And that prior fatigue, that desire to turn back and do nothing, defied even the sense of duty and the knowledge, confirmed time and again, that the first step was everything. Once combat was engaged, actions flowed with an amazing ease, almost without deliberation or any intervention of the will. And then the satisfaction of having done it, having overcome oneself before overcoming the enemy, made up for it all and stood as a precedent. But the precedent was no use, because the next time it was exactly the same.

At night, when Fulgentius was finally rid of tiresome centurions requiring guidance or asking tricky questions, he tried to silence his mind, to empty it of the sound and fury that had possessed it all day long. He knew from his reading that the gymnosophists, influenced by oriental charlatans, had developed techniques for achieving inner peace, which he wished he had been patient or gullible enough to learn. They would have come in handy in the present circumstances. After a day of violence and terror, he felt that his humanity had been drained and the tender shoots of his compassion trampled, that he had been shaped from without by the demon of brutality. That was not who he was; he had to find himself again. He called on the aid of darkness and henbane.

Perhaps it was a mistake to try to escape from reality and protect his inner life. Or so he thought, considering Lactarius, who threw himself into reality body and soul, merged his being with the circumstances, and was always happy. His inner life consisted of outward events, always new and colorful, with barely a pause for melancholy. But he was young. Fulgentius remembered being like that. With age he had succumbed to skepticism; the world had gradually withdrawn, leaving him alone, at the mercy of his thoughts.

By midday the battle was usually at its height. Luckily the weather was still cool; in midsummer heat it would have been a real sweat bath. Mounted on his white horse, Fulgentius surveyed the operations from the safety of the rearguard, making mental notes on the combat's shifting geometry. The blue of the sky had a yearning depth, which carried off the souls of the fallen. At one point, when the battle was raging, a wild boar ran onto the field, trampling whatever got in its way. It had clearly ended up there by mistake and was more frightened than the men who scattered before it. The creature's irrational confusion on finding itself at the center of something as rational as war expressed itself as blind fury, a state for which the species was admirably equipped. The battle came to a halt as the warriors on both sides, laughing and shouting, dodged the charging beast.

Observing these events from afar, Fulgentius, who never missed a chance to instruct his young lieutenant, said that back in the age of the early epics, the appearance of a wild boar would have been taken for an epiphany, the incarnation of a god: Mars for example, disobeying Jupiter's orders, avenging one of Venus's affairs, or some other similar fable. Homer specialized in those tall tales. Thankfully the epic had evolved, and poets no longer had to make fools of themselves pretending to believe in all that. But it wasn't just that Homer was a man of his benighted times, Fulgentius went on, he was mistaken for another reason too: since mythology was a kind of storytelling, it needed time to lay out its cadences and descriptions, its explanations of family relations and hierarchies, precedents, and wonders, all of which was incompatible with war, in which lives hung on a moment's action, and those digressions about the gods were absurdly out of place.

After three months of fierce combat and continuous Roman victories, the Pannonian forces were routed, and had withdrawn to Mursa, according to the intelligence that reached the legion. This was not good news. Mursa was a fortified city, with high walls, its own river, provisions supplied by seven farms and seven market gardens, and an incorruptible council. The Romans had known all this at the outset but had hoped to find the city weakened and ready to negotiate. The way things looked, it was quite the opposite. They would have their work cut out for them with the local militia, reinforced and fired up by the fanatical warriors driven down from the mountains. It was the legion that had been weakened; it was coming to the city burdened by the physical and mental fatigue of unremitting conflict. The reserves of energy built up over the winter were exhausted; the summer would be rainy, it seemed; the terrain they had to cross was rough, and getting there was barely the beginning of the problem.

This buildup of adversities led to a sharp drop in the general's spirits. He was already dragging his feet, weighed down by his philosophical pessimism; the prospect of a long siege, which might have meant months of immobility, seemed too much to bear. He took it personally. Why was this happening to him? He should have listened to his family and stayed at home. He was too old for these campaigns, which were nothing but trouble and strife. He chided himself for having naively presumed that he would be able to flit from city to city, staging his tragedy, with a few skirmishes here and there to keep up appearances. Nevertheless, the tragedy went with him, in his memory. During the endless marches, the verses that he had composed came back like a reverie. At other times they had sparked elation but now they disheartened him. He found the luxuriant vegetation of the Hyrcanian hills wearisome, almost irritating. Why did the trees have so many leaves? Did they really need them, or was it to show off or compete with the next tree—or just for the hell of it? It was the same with the hardships and problems that life served up so abundantly. He started taking medicinal herbs but his gloomy mood persisted.

Now and then, he defied the reasons of his heart by embarking on some project, as if to distract himself. Luckily, he wasn't short of ideas. For example, in a region abandoned by the resistance, he organized an opinion poll among the remaining locals. The aim was not to force them to talk at sword-point but to win their confidence with a show of good manners and consideration, some little gift or sex if necessary, in order to get them to open up. This had to be done by the rank and file, who could better empathize with the oppressed and downtrodden. Fulgentius worried, and with reason, that the task required a tact beyond the capacity of his battle-hardened men. But to his surprise, they followed the guidelines with a zeal that spoke of their hunger to do something other than kill. According to their findings, the rejection of the imperial invaders was by no means unanimous. Even if the results had been manipulated to please the general, there must have been some truth in them. It was the same everywhere: people were always looking for a new master, and if that master was the Lord of the World, they were bound to be better off.

Like all activities, this one came to an end, and apathy returned. How tired of living Fulgentius was! He withdrew to his tent. A legionary going to fetch him some chestnuts clumsily knocked over a cauldron full of a bubbling potion. Streams of orange milk ran over the ground in all directions. The general, who had taken off his sandals to rest his feet, picked them up and hung them on the bronze eagle's outstretched wings. He didn't rebuke the soldier. What was the point? It wouldn't make him mend his ways. The concoction was dubious anyhow; it had been brewed with herbs brought from Apulia, which had probably gone off. Also, there was a limit to the influence of the organic on the mental. He called for the haruspices and asked if they could interpret the patterns of the liquid on the ground, favorably if possible. They churlishly refused. He would have liked to be an oriental despot, who must be obeyed on pain of death. He ordered Lactarius to follow the dwarfs, who had rushed away on their bandy little legs muttering insults. The young man would have liked to refuse in turn, but he, at least, was subject to the general's will.

"I'll lose them. They're fast and slippery. Every time your Excellency orders me to follow them, I lose them and get lost myself."

"But how hard can it be to follow dwarfs?"

So the ill-starred days went by. How near or far the objective seemed depended on the fluctuating desire to reach it. The legion had a life of its own and moved at a constant speed, regardless of the general's moods.

They must have been closer to Mursa than he thought because a delegation soon came from the city. Fulgentius had to take his feet off the eagle and put on his sandals but he didn't fasten them. The emissaries asked him to march past the city without attacking it, so that they would have time to get rid of the refugees and, in due course, negotiate a separate peace. The mention of a separate peace made the general's blood run cold: nothing could be more dangerous in his view, not even war, but the proposal hinted at divisions within Mursa, which it made sense to exploit. In any case, they would have to attack and destroy, leaving not one stone upon another; it was the only way to tie up the mission without any loose ends. So Fulgentius dismissed the delegation with a rebuff and a threat. He gave them the dwarfs as a gift: a relief to him while landing them with a burdensome distraction.

Mursa appeared in the distance, shrouded in the vapors of a

torrid sunset. Its towers reared like natural rock formations; the marble of its temples set pink gleams along the crest of the city walls. For a long time as the soldiers marched toward the city, they nourished the hope that it was a mirage. It was too beautiful to be real. But real it was, and with every step they took, the beauty was transformed into ugliness. The city's prestige was due to its status as the gateway to southern Pannonia, a gateway that had the reputation of being permanently closed. The shepherds were returning with their flocks; the light was fading, and a cool breeze began to blow, promising some nocturnal relief from the sultriness of the day. A single arrow flew out of the city, its parabolic trajectory followed by six thousand pairs of eyes, and planted itself in front of the general's white horse. He called a halt and ordered his men to pitch camp. His voice rode on the sound of the arrow, whose muffled harmonics were still thrumming in the air.

Mursa fell, as all things do in life, especially when the agent bent on their fall is a legion of the Roman army. Fulgentius had foreseen no end of trouble, and his pessimism was justified. In fact it was overoptimistic. But afterward it all seemed unreal, and the many days of the offensive blurred into one another, forming a chaotic jumble like a dream. The only thing the general could remember clearly was how hopeless he had felt when anticipating what was to come. He couldn't leave that feeling behind. Wouldn't it be more practical, he wondered, to go straight to the end, when the task was completed and the problems solved and all that remained was the satisfaction of having finished? He didn't want to tie himself in a logical knot but he had a feeling that it wouldn't be so easy to skip the beginning.

He waited for the bodies to be removed before making his entry. The demolition took care of itself. Vermin and ivy would overrun the ruins of the city; for the moment it was an empty maze. Fulgentius toured it in silence with a small escort. The midday sun accentuated the desolation. The only people still walking the empty streets were the two dwarfs.

THE FALL OF MURSA OPENED UP ROUTES THAT HAD been closed to the Anatolian horse dealers. The restoration of trade would keep the survivors busy; soon the magnates would arrive, and their operations would guarantee peace by regulating time with schedules for payment in advance or arrears. The accelerations and immobilities of war would recede into the past. Those backward territories had to give up their culture of bartering and quartzite, and move to a scale economy, the kind that grips the mind like an obsession. The lords of the Capitol would earmark a huge mass of sesterces for column-by-column reconstruction, and that would lay the groundwork. The Wallachians, who had never seen a golden calf, would not know what to do with so much capital. Fulgentius, like all Romans of his generation, had something of the pregnant woman about him. Livy's onetime hobbyhorse, the Providential Man, was no longer the exception but the norm and therefore unremarkable: one might pass him on the street or even bump into him on the steps of the Forum without knowing who he was. Out there in the Balkan wilds he would be even easier to miss.

Fulgentius surveyed the scrubland and pictured a future of sumptuous tax revenue. Now that peace had come, the many baths in that thermally active region would reopen, and the senatorial matrons would flock there to cure their imaginary ailments and indulge in adultery. Looking back, he saw the fall of Mursa as a necessity; the fighting that had brought it down seemed like the stuff of dreams. The city's defenders must have known that it was the key to the region, and that was why they had chosen to die rather than hand it over, martyrs to an obsolete concept of economics.

"We're on the verge of a new flourishing," Fulgentius said to his officers as they gazed at the fallow land surrounding his white horse. And he quoted a line from Virgil: "It is the moment chosen by the plants to spring from the bosom of the earth."

The work of reconstruction began. Mursa would be rebuilt from scratch, under iron and marble laws, Roman down to its rats and ants. No more give-and-take autonomy. The Legate was everywhere at once, attending to organizational tasks. For a month he met with delegations from the various cities of the province, cracking the silken whip and the other one. There were mass migrations; territories were consolidated, and with the help of his own quaestors and others recruited for the task, a new tax table was drawn up. Fulgentius demanded a human tribute right away: men to work in the sulfur mines. He toiled from morning until night, virtually creating a new province. He even took account of women, who were generally ignored in practical demographics: he had their fertility assessed, distributed them accordingly, and confiscated their gold necklaces. The first consignments of goats were penned in yards built with cedar halberds, according to his orders. He inspected potential pastures and went so far as to chew on a weed and insist that Lactarius try it too, which led to an attack of colic. He barely slept and ate standing up, giving orders and gesticulating.

He was slightly overdoing it but in all sincerity. He wanted to prove to others and to himself that he was up to the role of statesman. A Roman general who took his duties seriously could not limit himself to killing. He had to kill, of course, and in fact internalize the image of himself as a killing machine, but once the corpses were piled high, he had to be able to map out the road to prosperity.

Fulgentius was well aware that everything he was doing out there in the wilds, in haste, before the dust of battle had settled, was makeshift, subject to revision, a draft. But if he wanted his statue in bronze to preside over the seat of administrative power, that draft, from the start, would have to possess whatever was needed to make it last. Or rather, it had to be a definitive draft. Work done in haste—under urgent, clashing pressures—could display the elegant carelessness of true talent, which doesn't fuss over refinements since a spontaneous hand can trace glorious curves that methodical craft could not achieve even by copying. That was the ideal he dreamed of; in practice he wore himself out patching things up here and there, going back, adding, revising if necessary. This or that part might have been a bit wobbly but he trusted that the whole would turn out well enough. Also, he knew for certain that the work, however bad, would be his, and the name and rank of

Fulgentius were in themselves guarantees of quality. He was the one who had brought down the walls; he was responsible for the noise each stone had made as it fell. Who else but he could carry out the reconstruction? If the first stage had unfolded like a dream, who but the dreamer could remember it?

Anxiety was growing in the capital, Sirmium. The general had decided to command operations from the field precisely to avoid interference by the province's central administration, which was thus kept at arm's length and reduced to executing orders. Cautious delegations came from the city, but he dismissed them brusquely with orders to prepare for the Triumph in two weeks' time. That was how long the city's theater troupe would have to rehearse his tragedy. He gave the scrolls to the delegates to pass on to the actors along with instructions for the staging. It would be the last production of the campaign, a self-awarded prize for his exploits. The play would have to be squeezed in between ceremonies. After some time off to enjoy the comforts of Sirmium, the legion would depart for Rome; the return could not be postponed any longer. The troops had been pushed to the limit over the one and a half years they had spent on the road and they were beginning to show signs of unrest.

It was always the same. Military life was ambivalent through and through. The men were happy to set off, to leave their domestic routines behind, and live unfettered like eternal bachelors. They relished in advance the license to kill, rape, and pillage. But they also anticipated the hardships of the march, the dangers of battle, the weariness, the hyperborean cold, and the sweltering Libyan heat. When the time came to return, it warmed their hearts to think of being home again, frequenting the same old tavern, going to the Coliseum on Sundays, exchanging the hobnailed sandal for the sympathetic slipper. But the heart's other ventricle grew cold as they remembered what also awaited them: the responsibilities of a father and a husband, the tedious in-laws, adjusting the family budget.

Fulgentius finally called a halt to the reconstruction, not because he was convinced that it had all been done in the best possible way but because he felt that he could go on finetuning indefinitely. "I could spend my whole life correcting," he thought. Faced with that prospect, he had to turn a blind eye and let the work take care of itself; the remaining imperfections would vanish into the whole. As opposed to war, in which each episode came to an objective end with a victory or a defeat, the projects of peacetime could only cease when someone decided to end them, whatever state they were in. And if they didn't turn out so well, there was always war to fix them up.

The day came. On a glorious sunny morning, the Lupine Legion, complete with standards, bronze eagles, wolfskin caps, and fierce martial gazes over neatly combed beards, made its entry into the city of Sirmium, to the delirious joy of the inhabitants, who hailed them as the saviors of Pannonia. Fulgentius, on his tall black horse, proceeded through a rain of flowers. The most desirable young women bared their breasts as he passed. The canticles were deafening; the children sported wolf costumes. Doves were released; the people cheered themselves hoarse ...

They were laying it on a bit too thick, out of remorse for their behavior during the conflict. As one of the cities that had the privilege of issuing imperial currency, Sirmium had been able to use money to hold off the threats, gladly submitting to all the extortion, which cost only a few extra hours of minting.

The legionaries played their part in these rituals with an obvious indifference. The Lupine Legion had been celebrated in a thousand Triumphs, some more deserved than others but always attended by enthusiastic crowds. It wasn't simply habit, however, that was dulling their emotions. They didn't feel like heroes because there was something unreal about the battles they had fought, which were fading from their memories like dreams. Since the legion was a mobile apparatus, each thing it did was done in a different place: there was no time to build up a sense of reality. Only the winter months, which they had spent quartered by the frozen lake, might have left them something solid to remember, but that long crepuscular spell of snow and fog had been the most fantastic of all. Remembering it would have been like composing a poetic scene in the mind, and nothing could have been more alien to the legionary's practico-mechanical mindset.

Sirmium, the historical capital of Pannonia, had reinvented and modernized itself. The city had come a long way from its Illyrian and Celtic origins. The riches on display were comparable to those to be seen in any of the empire's great capitals. It was the seat of a Praetorian Prefecture. The river Sava, which ran through the city, was crossed by elaborately engineered bridges. It would have taken more than a year to visit all the monuments, temples, and mausoleums, to say nothing of the mansions of the wealthy merchants, surrounded by gardens with fountains and imported statues. A crowded agenda left Fulgentius little opportunity to appreciate these beauties and riches. In their overzealous desire to please, the locals gave him not a moment's peace. In the consular palace the full complement of praetorian officials came to greet him in a slow file. There were laurel wreaths for everyone, winged Victories performing the customary dances, beads of Pergamon glass, incense, hand-kissing. The corridors of the Temple of Wisdom, with their caldarium and frigidarium, had been set aside for the general's personal use, but his slave boy had more leisure to enjoy them. Fulgentius summoned the centurions and told them to order the men not to pitch camp: they would be leaving the following day. There were reasons for his haste. His policy in big cities had been to promise a long stay, which prevented the men from disgracing themselves in the first two or three days: they put it off, reckoning that there would be time for their outrages later on, when the locals had lowered their guard. For those three days, they behaved like gentlemen, while secretly sharpening their claws; on the fourth, Fulgentius would abruptly announce that he had changed his mind and issue marching orders. This was terribly frustrating for the legionaries but letting them indulge their basest instincts was out of the question. The ruse had worked on more than one occasion, but its victims had begun to wise up, so this time the general decided that they wouldn't stay even for those three days. They would leave at dawn and that was that.

"But your Excellency . . ." complained the centurions, who had to face the men. They argued that the city was full of elegant courtesans, distilled beverages, loins of venison: "And when will they ever get a chance to return to a place so far away?"

Fulgentius stood firm. He contrasted the city's dubious charms with those of the journey ahead: the delicate Carpathian autumn, the rivers and mountains, the Lamias of the passes, Rome on the horizon. The debate went no further, in part because the general was not about to let reason outweigh authority but also because a committee came to fetch him for the banquet. He left Lactarius and the slave boy splashing around in the baths and went off stoically.

He had seen the Proconsul Marius at the Triumph; now the man latched onto him and remained at his side throughout the rest of the day's ceremonies and celebrations, which his company made all the more exhausting. No doubt he had been chosen for the job of minder because of his confident, man-of-the-world manner, his nonstop conversation, and perhaps his lack of aptitude for any other task. His virtues made him unbearable. He didn't give the visitor's ears a moment of respite. Like many men of his ilk, he had no idea how to behave, as indicated by a story that he told during the meal.

It was about the visit of an envoy from Rome, sent to Sirmium some time before to check the accounts. A banquet had been organized for him, similar to the one at which the story was told, and everything was going well until the officials noticed that among the guests was a civil prefect, whom they had been careful not to invite, because they knew that he had expressed an intention to denounce certain accounting irregularities. That would have been embarrassing for everyone. By some oversight on the part of the doorkeepers, he had managed to slip in. Immediate action had to be taken. No messing around: they poisoned his drinking cup. But in the haste of the moment they used a slow-acting poison, which would need a good half hour, at least, to take effect. And the man, it seemed, was about to talk; in fact he was already attracting the inspector's attention. With meaningful looks the guests urged each other to keep him quiet, ranging over various topics, drawing out the conversation with an interesting digression, then switching to a new subject, or a joke, or a song ...

The Proconsul couldn't stop laughing as he told the story. How they racked their brains in search of noisy distractions, wearing their voices out with speeches that grew more and more incoherent, motivated only by the need to stop someone else from speaking! And all the while glancing surreptitiously at the victim to see if he had finally keeled over.

"He held out for ages, the bastard! We were beginning to think we'd given him a tonic instead of poison. And we were running out of conversation topics! What a fix, ha ha ha!"

When it came to the dénouement, Fulgentius was appalled. In the end, the poor wretch fell down dead, and that gang of cretins breathed a sigh of relief. The anecdote was hardly edifying but it was also supremely tactless, the general thought, since there he was, at the scene of the crime, with a bowl of wine in his hand. And this was just one of the verbal assaults that he had to endure at the hands of his assigned companion.

The rest of the afternoon was given over to meetings, reviewing the guard, and the presentation of parchments. On behalf of the troops, the centurions appealed to Fulgentius once again to delay the departure. He held firm. The mere thought of being subjected to the Proconsul's chatter for a week made his flesh creep.

The decision to leave immediately imposed a sacrifice on him too, since his curious and cultivated mind could have profited from the art and architecture of Sirmium. But those visits to famous cities, however extended, were never long enough. And, in their way, they were grueling. You had to choose what to see, because you could never see it all, and apportion the available time in the most efficient manner, which led to worries and regrets, and in the end the distress outweighed the enjoyment. Not to mention the exhaustion that followed those days of rushing around. And you could never be sure that you had made the right decisions: if you went to the places of greatest renown, others that were more obscure might have been more interesting (and vice versa).

As night was falling the general's hosts escorted him to the amphitheater where the gala performance of his tragedy was to take place. He was impressed by the magnificence of the edifice, which could hold twelve thousand spectators. It was full. Half the city had turned out, attracted by a shrewd publicity campaign, which had stressed how exceptional it was for a Roman general to write a tragedy, especially an autobiographical one, and for the work to be performed in his presence. The Proconsul Marius (who else?) sat down beside Fulgentius in the middle of the fourth row, verbiage tripping off his silver tongue. He extolled the Legate's popular appeal: it was impressive to have drawn such a crowd on the day of a chariot-racing final.

The performance was excellent, the best that Fulgentius had seen that year. It was almost too good for his liking, since he had developed a taste for the chancy and the eccentric. In this case everything was done in strict conformity to the rules of the art, with professional actors, gold-embroidered tunics, old helmets set with precious stones, and a chorus trained to articulate perfectly. The actor playing the lead role had an imposing stage presence and the voice of a wolf trainer. Fulgentius was flattered to see himself in such a form but he wondered if it might not make him seem less human. Everything suggested that the sycophants of Sirmium were trying to portray him as a demigod, although he would have preferred to come across as a wavering tragic hero at the mercy of fate. These and other objections occurred to him during the opening scenes but were soon swept aside when, as always, he was drawn into the unfolding work. And, as always, he repeated the verses to himself along with the actors, barely moving his lips this time so the Proconsul sitting beside him wouldn't notice. Had Marius been more observant, however, he would have noticed all the same, since a little nod of the general's head marked each of the four stresses in every hexameter.

The actors' voices rose above the silent multitude that covered the amphitheater like a human forest on a mountainside. The encroaching dark enriched the atmosphere with an element essential to tragedy: imminence. The doves that were perched in compact rows along the top wall seemed to be paying attention.

With each successive passage, the general's exaltation intensified. The work's deep meaning took hold of him in a peculiar, intense, and almost painful way. It had been worth laying waste to a province to experience that emotion. He supposed that it was partly due to the thought, on which he chose not to dwell, that he might be hearing his tragedy for the last time. There would be no stopovers on the journey back to Rome, and it was unlikely that he would be given command of another campaign. Other opportunities would arise, he felt sure, but the sense of an ending persisted. And it touched on something more remote: the sense of a beginning. Remote, but very present too, because it was right there in front of him, on stage, captured by the tragedy that he had written so many years before, in the springtime of his life. What a tremendous stroke of luck it had been that the boy Fulgentius, with his smooth pink cheeks and blond curls, had taken up his stylus to compose the portrait of a life to come.

People had sometimes asked him why he had not continued to write, after such a precocious and promising debut. Which showed that they had completely missed the point; they were treating him as if he were a mere writer, as if all that could be expected of him was that he would go on producing work. Not that he had anything against writers and poets, whether epic or tragic. On the contrary he admired them, but he was not one of their number. That was why when he talked to the young he abstained from advising them to do things. Although he shared the common opinion that "young people who get things done" are investing in the future, he also saw a risk: the things might turn out well enough to make the young want to go on doing them, and then they would be set on a career, a fixed path from which there would be no escape. With the added drawback that they would never be able to match the quality of the first thing they had done.

His own case was different and so unique it frightened him. Without any vanity (or barely as much as one needs to keep going), he felt like a man apart. It was as if the death of his character at the threshold of his adult life had projected him into another dimension. The ritual repetition of that death and the tears he had shed for it, over and over, had produced a distancing effect, transforming the real Fulgentius into a lone star on the black stage of the sky.

The Proconsul Marius, who had initially observed a respectful silence, was unable to keep it up for long. Not even the most basic rules of politeness could restrain his verbal incontinence.

He began with sporadic interjections—"so good" and "so interesting"—but then elaborated until the flow of words was
continuous. Although annoyed, Fulgentius could not ignore
him entirely; his attention was split between Marius and the
stage. "What but misguided politeness," he wondered, "is stopping me from sending him to Orcus?" But he turned it into a
challenge, a matter of personal pride: steering his conscious-
ness in two opposite directions without any loss of intensity.
There was inevitably some loss, however, since what Marius
had to say was not devoid of interest. The man was a jerk, but a
clever jerk. If he had been talking pure nonsense, it would have
been easy to disregard him and turn a deaf ear to his chatter. His
comments showed that he knew the play well: he must have attended the rehearsals or looked over the scrolls; windbags of
his sort typically had a finger in every pie. It was a new experience for the author to be viewing the action against the background of another spectator's comments, however far-fetched.

"Sometimes I forget you're sitting beside me; I see you there
on stage, tangling with those wicked Scythians, and I fear for
your safety. But then I turn and see you sitting here perfectly
calm, enjoying the show. This doubling reminds me of something that happened to me yesterday at siesta time, when I was
asleep I mean, because if I don't take an hour's nap after lunch,
I'm no good for anything in the afternoon. No, no, don't worry,
I'm not going to bore you to death by telling you a dream. I'll
only tell you the relevant parts, two little bits, that's all. So my
oldest friend appeared in the dream, and I should explain that

he has lost a lot of hair; he's not completely bald, but he's getting there. We're almost the same age; he's a year older than me, but I still have almost all my hair; the hairline has just receded a little, as you can see. The thing is, in the dream, my friend had a luxuriant head of hair, dark and curly, with a great big cowlick on his forehead. I thought: 'He's put on a wig. How odd that a man of such refinement (he's a poet) should resort to something so obvious, and choose such an over-the-top hairpiece, as if he'd suddenly become immune to ridicule.' Then, at another moment in the dream, I ran into him again; he was still wearing a wig, but now it was more discreet, not so voluminous, and suddenly, with a start, I remembered something, and said to him: 'Arcturus, you're not going to believe this but a little while ago I dreamed of you, and here we are bumping into each other for the first time in a year!' I tactfully neglected to mention the wig, although it was the most striking premonition in the dream."

"A dream within a dream."

"Which is what this play of yours reminds me of, folding reality into the unreal, creating an invagination by virtue of your double presence ..."

He went on like that all through the performance, superimposing stories on the story. This distraction could not make the general lose a plot he knew inside out. But it did open an empty space between him and the work and allow him to see it from a new point of view. In spite of his long experience as an author-spectator, he was still learning. Until then he had always assumed that identification was the only way to engage with his tragedy. But there was another way, which he could not have discovered without making the long journey to Sirmium and getting stuck with an overarticulate Proconsul. It was true that this divided and therefore distant listening broke with theatrical convention, but it allowed him to notice subtleties that would have been drowned out by the pathos of outright identification. He felt this particularly at the moment of his death, when for the first time he was able to hold back his tears and replace them with a more intellectual response.

Death on stage was not, as people said, a caricature of that ultimate formality. True, when the play was over, the dead got up and went home, or retired to the tavern, cracking jokes. But their survival did not invalidate the deaths that they had acted out. Death was an event that had only half an existence, if that: one of its halves was superreal and full of action, but the other was completely empty. The second, dark half could be set aside as nonexistent, so it made no difference whether its subjects were lying cold and stiff in a grave or going to the tavern to drink with their friends.

When the play was over, the conversation continued unavoidably, and Fulgentius discovered that he had almost come around to Marius. After all, the man was affable and well-meaning; he couldn't help being incorrigible. And his interest in the Legate seemed sincere. He had questions to pose but first he apologized, saying that he had never had the chance to discuss a literary work with its author.

"I would have liked to talk like this with Aeschylus or Sophocles."

"I don't deserve the honor of being compared with the giants," said Fulgentius.

"They were just examples. I didn't mean to compare," Marius replied with a disarming sincerity.

His doubts revolved around the notion of autobiography. How much truth, how much of the author's own experience was there in this story about a star-crossed romance with a princess of the steppes, the assassination of a barbarian king, and the hero's death at the hands of a hunchback? As far as Marius knew, the general was a respectable family man, a stranger to adultery, and a disciplined military officer who had never ventured beyond the bounds of the empire or stabbed a king of any sort. Also, he was alive and well.

For a moment, Fulgentius weighed up the possibility of telling him the truth, which was that he had scribbled down willy-nilly whatever he could fit into the hexameter's iron mold. If he were to tell Marius that, he could also tell him that he had written the play as a boy, before experience had acquainted him with the gray, conventional, boring facts of real life, which were not worth writing about. But such revelations were out of the question. It was a part of the poet's work, an integral part, to preserve the mystery, even if it meant lying. So he replied with a conspiratorial air that it was a coded tragedy. The look on the face of his interlocutor revealed that the concept was new to him. Which didn't surprise Fulgentius, since he had just ex-

tracted the concept in question from the overflowing cornuco-
pia of his imagination.

"What it means is that every real act, every person, is represented faithfully but in a different form. Imagine I want to tell
the story of how I picked up a dry leaf from the ground" (saying
this, he picked up a yellow leaf that had fallen from one of the
Egyptian sycamores on either side of the entrance to the amphitheater), "but I don't want people to know what I did, so I
write that I looked up into the night sky and saw a star."

It was true that the leaf was vaguely star-shaped. The proconsul did not seem particularly impressed by the example.

"And why would you want to hide something as innocent as
having picked up a leaf?"

"It was just an example. And besides, you never know. The
most innocent act can turn out to be the most compromising
of all."

"But isn't that procedure a bit mechanical?"

"So? What's wrong with that?"

"I don't know ... Anyway. It must be fun."

"It's more than fun. Those substitutions are what give the
world its variety and charm."

The conversation was interrupted by the arrival of the praetorian prefect and the other senior officials, who had been at
the hippodrome. The proconsul lost no time in asking about
the race, and to judge from the avidity with which he drank in
the results, it must have been a great sacrifice for him to rep-
resent the government at the amphitheater. Perhaps he had

drawn the short straw, and they had sent him to sit through a boring tragedy so as not to offend the important visitor.

The favor that the officials had to ask of Fulgentius was important too. They must have been deliberating and even vacillating, because they had left it until the last minute. It was a delicate matter, involving purely juridical reasons of state and the legal latitudes permitted in the farther provinces. Sirmium, situated at the center of a geological basin rich in metals, was, as mentioned already, the site of a major mint. Aurei and denarii, rivers of sesterces and oceans of assarii were struck there for all the business transactions from Hispania to Chaldea, from rainy Britannia to scorching Libya. The city's economy was based on the manufacturing of money, whose purity was therefore safeguarded with the utmost vigilance. A problem had arisen in the previous year, as alarming as it was foreseeable: counterfeiting. Because the coins were so well forged, the authorities preferred to let them circulate, rather than alerting the public and creating distrust, which is the worst thing that can happen to a currency. Luckily, they had been able to put a stop to the operation, shutting down the secret workshop and doing away with all those involved: a series of discreet executions at midnight had disposed of the craftsmen and distributors, and even the men who had swept up the bronze filings. A problem arose, however, when they identified the head of the gang. He was a patrician from an eminent family, well connected both in the province and in Rome. The fraud had been his idea, and he had pulled it off well enough to rock an institution as solid

as the Sirmium Mint. A genius. Of the evil variety, alas. Since
the whole operation had been kept secret, and it would have
been dangerous to uncover it while the convincing sesterces
were still in circulation, the counterfeiter couldn't be tried or
put to death without an explanation. The solution they had
come up with was to pretend that he was going on a trip, and
the presence of the Lupine Legion, passing through on its way
back to Rome, supplied them with the perfect cover, as long as
General Fulgentius agreed. Would he be able to transport the
delinquent, under strict guard, to a certain point along the way?

"I see no reason why not," replied the Legate, "but why to a
certain point and not all the way to Rome? And what point?"

The subprefect threw the proconsul a glance that might have
meant, "He's so slow."

They were obliged to spell it out. Which they did with the
appropriate euphemisms and complicit smiles. The idea was
that the person in question would not arrive in Rome, or anywhere in fact, but disappear along the way as if by magic, in
some precipitous corner of the picturesque Alps, for example,
and nothing more would ever be heard of him. In Rome, his
relatives would think he was still in Sirmium; his friends in Sirmium would be sure that he was in Rome, having seen him set
off for that destination. The slowness and precarity of com-
munications, a cause of continual complaint, would provide
a handy excuse for the silence. And eventually people would
forget.

SUMMER WAS IN ITS FINAL THROES WHEN THE LEGION set off through the woods and meadows to the south of Sirmium on its way back to Rome. The route they chose was slightly longer than the one they had taken on the outward journey but it spared them having to see the destruction they had wrought along the way. The calendar dictated a moderate haste, if they were to cross the alpine passes before the snow set in. But the march was fairly leisurely and the weather clement. The men went hunting and unwound in the natural swimming pools. They marked their passage with wedge-shaped altars, which they built by the roadside with stones and instant mortar. Every five days they took a day of rest. The carts were loaded with treasures and curiosities from the strange lands they had visited. Their arms were idle; the gladius was used only to cut the throats of little wild pigs, not much bigger than a large rat: a parasitic species hosted by the Sow, considered extinct and soon to be so. The Sow would have to make do without them.

Fulgentius discovered this and other facts about the local fauna, in which he had previously shown no interest, from Maximus, the counterfeiter for whose captivity and transport he was now responsible. Scorning the rather obsessive precautions that had been urged upon him in Sirmium, he did not place the prisoner under guard or keep him in chains. The man had been dangerous as a source of false currency but out in the open, under the blue skies of Dalmatia, he could do no harm; nor could he escape, since in those vast deserted spaces the legion exerted an irresistible gravitational force.

Fulgentius was curious: he kept the prisoner close in order to sound him out and was surprised to find that Maximus was a cultivated and polite interlocutor. Prejudice against lawbreakers had led him to expect some kind of brute, but he should have remembered that this was a gentleman criminal. He was irresistibly drawn to the prisoner, captivated by what he had to say. It was so rare to find someone who could hold up his end of a serious conversation through a long day's march. With Lactarius it was like talking to oneself; for all his good will, the poor boy was always coming up against his intellectual limitations. From Maximus, on the other hand, the general could expect a genuine response, and more.

There was indeed something more: the tried and tested attraction of opposites. It was bound to come into play between two such dissimilar men: on the one hand, a Roman general, a model of probity; on the other, a scoundrel who had dared to undermine society's most sacred institution. The abyss of Evil held fabulous secrets that Fulgentius had always longed to explore. And haunting the cornices of that abyss, the great counterfeiter felt an equally keen curiosity. He wondered how it was possible to remain honest when plotting crimes was the only real way to exercise intelligence.

As the vistas of the journey spilled a profusion of treasures

before them, the Legate came to appreciate the company of his
unwilling guest more and more. So much in fact that he pro-
cured a horse tall enough to raise the captive to his own level so
that they could converse comfortably. Which was no mean feat,
because the general's big white steed was a veritable equine giant. With a newcomer's puzzlement, Maximus inquired:

"I've heard people mention your big black horse and your
big white horse, and I'm confused by the contradiction. Is it
black or white? Or are there two horses?"

This question, which no one had ever put to him, convinced Fulgentius that he was dealing with a truly intelligent
man, someone who knew how to tell the difference between
words and images. After long months of sharing his days with
men who based all their thoughts on the evidence of the senses,
Fulgentius was delighted by the change. The fellow was like-
able right from the start. He was a true Roman, a fine figure of
a man, about the same age as the Legate, with a manner that
stopped just short of haughtiness. The intelligence that shone
in his face had enabled him to accumulate a vast amount of
knowledge, a store that inspired the general's growing and awe-
struck admiration. Fulgentius came to the conclusion that this
man had used intelligence as almost no one else had done: to
find out more. It seemed the obvious thing to do and yet it was
vanishingly rare. The vast majority of those with a functioning
mind were content simply to be so endowed: they were satisfied with its latent power and feared that activating it might
lead to deterioration. They used it only when they had to, for

solving problems. Fulgentius had belonged to that silent majority, and the revelation that he had been granted was like the discovery of a continent.

Maximus neither showed off nor concealed his knowledge: when the occasion arose, he knew how to share it in a polite and pleasant way, whether it related to the name and properties of a plant seen by the wayside, a word's Aramaic root, the geological structure of the mountains they were crossing, the history of the Etruscans and their forgotten deeds, or the anatomy of the inner ear. He could recite long passages from Archilocus in Greek, and Celtic spells in the mellifluous tongue of the Druids.

When they halted for the night and unsaddled, the conversation continued, touching on subjects beyond the realm of direct experience, which seemed especially well suited to the intimacy of darkness. Geometry, for example, the still dance of the polyhedra, whose dimensions were all-important, and yet they could be set aside and nothing would be changed. There was no such thing as a form without sides, but there were sides without form. Planes were defined by color, the circle by the fine legs on which it stood, if it happened to be a little round table. And intimately related to solid geometry: optics. A beam from a light source could be seen to waver in the smoke given off by a hot plate. How could one trap the white fire of lightning? How could vibrations be dampened? There was an answer to everything.

On rest days, they botanized, for no practical purpose,

moved by the pure love of differences. No two blades of grass were identical, no two leaves had the same vein structure; the universe of forms was like the world of human dreams. Along the river banks they found agates which, once cut and polished, revealed the shapes secreted within them by fickle tectonic forces. Maximus explained the reactions that led to the formation of the forms, and Fulgentius listened with his mouth agape. He was discovering that the visible was the mere tip of the invisible. And that everything had an explanation, whether or not it needed one.

The flight of birds, and of bats, which emerged from their caves in dense flocks, wing to wing. The notes of a song in the night, the Lydian mode. The persistence of flowers, brittle schists, furry and furless animals, bubbles inhabiting water. All these enumerations, and many others, were implicit. Some links found verbal form, others remained mere promises, mist, soft approximations of thought.

Needless to say, the two men became inseparable. Fulgentius delegated all practical matters to a group of trusted centurions so as to make the most of his new friend's instructive company, which he knew was destined not to last. Lactarius was jealous and shadowed them for a while but he was so bored by their talk about basalt, frogs, and Hittites that he soon went back to his dice and dyes.

"What do I care how dwarfs used to comb their hair?" he grumbled aloud, not minding who heard, referring to the prisoner's digressions about the various kinds of braiding used by primitive humans, who were still poorly formed, to distinguish women from men.

Lactarius couldn't understand how the general, who had overseen his own education in military matters and in life, could be taken in by that charlatan and his spiel. He thought he knew Fulgentius but there was no knowing one's fellow man well enough to be safe from surprises, it seemed.

As for the general, he would not have understood his young protégé's resentment. He considered the pageant of knowledge to be suitable for all. Since it was all-embracing, it could satisfy all tastes. The supply was generous. Too generous, perhaps?

"Isn't it presumptuous," he wondered, "to want to fathom it all? Mightn't it lead to anxiety about how little one can really know?"

"Not at all," replied Maximus, with the serene authority that always accompanied his smile. "The unfathomable surrenders its treasures just like the fathomable."

The man was never lost for an answer. New avenues of learning were opening up before Fulgentius. At night they moved away from the campfires ("There go the sweethearts," said the legionaries, looking up from their dice for a moment), retired behind a thicket or a rock in search of perfect darkness and contemplated the starry sky. Maximus could read it like the pages of a book. He showed Fulgentius the measureless abysses that served to ground perspective, and the triangulations of distance. As distinct from the world in which they stood, where everything could be taken lightly because it was all transient, the ceremonies of the stars above them were no joking matter. A gleam appeared in the general's suddenly dreamy pupils as he glimpsed the possibility of a world where all that was said would be said in all seriousness. And he let the sound of his companion's calm voice carry him up and away to the colossal pyramids of black ether.

Arm in arm, as night fell over the mountains, they walked on paths invented by their steps. The unchanging presence of the trees, the constancy of the horizons, the ironic immortality of the birds all seemed like intellectual exercises. When Maximus, modestly declining praise, said that knowledge, in the end, was no more than a replica of the real world, Fulgentius suddenly remembered, as if waking from a nap, that everything surrounding him was real. It had been necessary to replicate reality to get it out from under the glass.

"Shall we head back? I'm curious to taste that sautéed quail the cook was promising."

"Yes, I'm starting to feel peckish."

"Life in the open air awakens the healthiest part of our animal nature, don't you think?"

After the meal they would count stars.

Just as he read the skies above, Maximus could read human dreams, those other dark skies thronged with bodies at least as intriguing and far away as those of the firmament. He seemed to possess the secret key to the trove of stories that had nourished human imagination for countless centuries. And what came to light in his conversation or his answers to questions were the chanced-upon outcrops of an enormous mass made up of all the forms and colors of the world. The superfine pink scale of a fish, the iridescence of its underside, and its imperceptible outline corresponded to the march of armies across continents, the fall of legendary kingdoms, the longing of a virgin. Everything existed in the memory of one man. Or that, at least, is how it seemed to Fulgentius in his dazzled awe. No one could call him mediocre, if as the old Roman proverb said: "To admire with moderation is a sign of mediocrity."

After this bout of hyperbole, on further reflection he found even more to admire. Maximus was a universal man, although not a genius. He must have been predisposed to knowledge, gifted but not exceptionally so. Endowed with a good, retentive memory, and intelligence, but perhaps no more richly than others. He might even have begun with average gifts. But the rest was his own work. His great merit had been knowing how to use his time. The time that slipped through most people's fingers like barren sand to be whisked away by the wind had been an instrument for him, a lectern on which to rest his books. He had also known how to make the most of the opportunities provided by the era and place in which he had been born. There too he furnished a proof of his exceptional character. Most people abstained from cultivating their minds on the indisputable grounds that civilization would continue to progress, so there would be more information and knowledge in the future. Why bother to store up learning that would soon become obsolete? They used that fallacious argument as an excuse not to study the culture available in the present.

A seed had been sown in the Legate's mind. He still didn't

know what it was; he was still too blinded by his fascination with Maximus. But more than once, on hearing the captive relate a fact or an explanation, he wondered if he hadn't known it already. How could I not have known that? he thought. And yet it felt new. He supposed that the impression was caused by knowing and having repeatedly used all the words in which the knowledge had been expressed. It was the combination that was new. But that combination was latent in the words.

The seed germinated in a moment of solitude as Fulgentius gazed at the vast rocky membranes of the Alps. The wind cried out in the gorges; the violets raised their purple heads, and the snow's glaring white persisted on the retina. In a kind of slow respiration, the legion spread itself out from horizon to horizon during the day, contracting at night to a compact mass of bodies huddled together. The sunlight had become more intense; luminous air filled the general's lungs, and a note of enthusiasm sounded in his mind.

He had hatched the idea of being his own Maximus. It was the idea of universal knowledge, which his captive had put into practice. With Maximus gone, Fulgentius realized that what he had done was to expel the idea from himself, the better to contemplate it in the person of another. Now he drew it back in with an implosive systole, and it was as if the upside-down world had been righted once again.

The possibility opening up before him was infinite. To study, to learn, to become a new Pliny, not in order to get rich or show off, but for the inner satisfaction of being a hero of the intellect. He could draw a line under his army career. He had done enough for the empire and had no desire to go on razing and seizing for the benefit of idle, parasitic courtiers, who used the provincial taxes to finance their leisure activities. At one stroke he would banish the thousand frustrations born of imperfectly occupied time and hampered intentions, since from now on he would always have something to do, something interesting by definition.

It was largely because of his character and training that he could see this as a possibility. His military career had accustomed him to discipline, method, and planning. But all the discipline, method, and planning that a soldier put into his work came up against the enemy's stubborn resistance, whereas the scholar, in splendid isolation, could glory in a virtual omnipotence.

The change of lifestyle was enough to validate the project. He realized that his life in the service of the legions had been a long series of delays. What was war itself but waiting for it to be over? The campaigns of learning, on the other hand, would occupy time without leaving any gaps, because they would all blend into one. They would merge with time and fill it as water fills a cavity, however irregular. Best of all, nothing would be lost. In other areas of experience, one had to choose between the useful and the futile, and there were so many more things in the second category that the first seemed empty in the end. But for an explorer of knowledge, everything was useful: the merest trifle—a stone, a letter, a cough—could be the point of departure for a new adventure in thought. And the handler of this wealth took up an active stance, which was something new and refreshing for a military man, obliged by the real or imaginary presence of the enemy to remain passive or reactive if he were not to perpetrate gratuitous aggression or violence.

There was a touch of vanity in this desire to become the sort of cultural hero whose every word is treasured by listeners gaping in admiration. But there was no risk of vanity taking over: given how little attention his fellow citizens paid to culture, few would gape, or even bother to listen to what he said. He was more strongly motivated, if much more subconsciously, by the desire to place himself above the claims of domestic life.

He was excited by the project. He wondered why it hadn't occurred to him before. What was the world for if not to be absorbed by thought and used to build beautiful castles, interesting stories, and poetry? His good cheer began to show. He rode with his head in the clouds, designing his future, and the smile on his lips was sometimes transformed into laughter or an exclamation, when he remembered botany, or the chronology of the Olympic Games, waiting to supply him with more and better things to do.

Although used to his changes of mood, the legionaries were intrigued. The conjectures that they tossed around all fell wide of the mark. They realized that he had reasons to be happy: he was returning home safe and sound, having concluded a successful campaign, received all manner of honors from the Pannonian sycophants, and treated himself to the pleasure of inflicting his tragedy on half the known world. But this was all within the normal range of a Roman general's life satisfaction; and there was something more, they could tell, that was tickling his soul, something he was keeping to himself.

They turned to Lactarius, who had recovered his place at the general's side. The young man was happy to be the favorite again but slightly resented the weeks of exclusion. He had no special insight into what was making Fulgentius so happy. He grew impatient with the men who questioned him as the Legate's longtime confidant. Lying shamelessly, he declared that as soon as they got back to Rome, he would look for another position and get away from the "crazy old guy."

What he didn't know was that Fulgentius was, at that very moment, building him into his plans. On the premise that teaching was the best way to learn, he would take Lactarius as his pupil. For a start, he would teach him Greek, which would be useful for brushing up his own rather rusty skills in that language. Likewise with other subjects: the lad would serve a useful purpose, as he had failed to do so far; he would be the general's study aid.

Practical to the core, Fulgentius did not allow his dreams of wisdom to distract him from the concrete circumstances required for their realization. He would have to find himself a study where he could set up his library and work in peace. The most convenient solution would be to build a separate pavilion in the grounds of his villa on the Aventine Hill. And he would have to hire tutors for the languages that he proposed to learn; in a cosmopolitan city like Rome, they wouldn't be hard to find (or expensive: they'd be desperate for work). And there would be scientific instruments to buy, although he didn't yet know what they might be. Before any of this he would have to build up a library from scratch: he had nothing. He knew from having ordered copies of his tragedy that scrolls were very dear, and the scope of his plan meant that he would need thousands.

At this point, he realized that the cost of the enterprise was a problem. His general's pension, although generous, barely sufficed to cover the household expenses, what with all the servants his wife required, his parasitic in-laws, and his children's artistic pretensions, untainted by hope of gain.

The solution, however, was within reach. Given the prestige of his rank and the strings he could pull, it wouldn't be hard for him to secure one of those honorary posts taken on by disinterested, community-minded patricians who declared their nostalgia for the Republic and used their new appointments to set up lucrative business deals. He had always disdained such stratagems, but the time had come to set excessive scruples aside. In one of those roles, he could sell slave importation licenses at sky-high prices and demand a commission. It was illegal but if Agamemnon had sacrificed his beloved daughter in order to go to Troy, Fulgentius could sacrifice an honesty that nobody had asked him to exercise—much less thanked him for—in pursuit of an objective more worthy than a war. Also, he was sure that as he advanced in his knowledge of other cultures, he would discover one, or several, in which the concept of honesty did not exist. From time to time, a healthy dose of relativism was just the thing to free up those awkward rigidities that were always hampering action.

He made no attempt to hasten the march, although he could have done so. Since he felt that he was bound for a whole new life, a week's delay seemed negligible. He was relishing the anticipation so much he barely noticed the landscape; he was already immersed in his future. He missed out on the smiling white half-moon in the blue morning sky, the winding of the paths, the rippled brook, and the calm, firm footfalls of the men. He couldn't stop them killing a beautiful snake; his distraction licensed their iniquities.

The first blackbird flinging out garbled words meant that they had reached their homeland. Once again they tasted vegetables watered by the rains they knew so well. The little villages of the plain continued with their work as they watched the soldiers marching by. Mounted on his big black horse, sporting his absent smile, Fulgentius attracted attention. He wouldn't have been the first general to be declared Emperor by his legionaries and march on Rome to uphold his claim with blood and fire. Nothing could have been further from the truth in this case. The possession that he was planning to take, which lit up the route before him in broad daylight, was as private as the workings of an internal organ.

Rome, with its hills and marble, the white nightmare of the world, lay hidden still beyond the horizon, but they could already sense its proximity. Something like a shock ran through the columns of men-at-arms. The general's enthusiasm, fueled by the imminence of arrival, was swirling in his head. How short-lived it would turn out to be, poor man! He felt he was already home ... Soon it would be time to begin ...

Thoughts of his home and family life, which wrested him from the fantasy world of encyclopedic erudition that he had conjured up, and the thought of "beginning," above all, acted upon him like a cerebral frigidarium. Under the effect of that verb, *incipio* (I begin), the cold solidified as ice, and the ice broke with an ominous crack that dissipated the dream. He had suddenly remembered that he was sixty-seven years old (and in a month, as soon as he got back to Rome, he would turn sixty-eight). Could he really start something new at that age? Something modest perhaps: a cabbage patch or a rabbit hutch, to mention just two kinds of food that he hated, but not the encyclopedic study of languages, arts, philosophy, and history. What had he been thinking? A project of that magnitude required the freshness and vigor of youth. Even if he managed, by sheer force of will, to produce a reasonable imitation of freshness and vigor (how pathetic!), there was a more decisive obstacle, over which he had no control: time, the years he no longer had before him for the raising of his great edifice.

When he compared what he was to what he might have become, he felt that his life had been one long waste of time. Like the artificial time of the theater. Perhaps his passion for watching time and time again the tragedy that he had written in his youth was a vain attempt to recover a real time. The project of appropriating all the variety of the world through knowledge had been equally vain. Surrendering that dream, as he was doing, giving in to common sense, was the start, he could tell, of a series of surrenders that would last all his remaining days.

Just as well he hadn't told anyone! How ridiculous: an old man going to school. He sank into a backward-looking silence, chastened by uneasy feelings of emptiness and remorse.

As the days of marching went by, he gradually recovered his peace of mind. He tried to convince himself that it had been just another bad idea, one of many. He had to press on and forget it. But forgetting was also a part of the sadness. His spirits sank into apathy, where they remained. The legionaries couldn't help noticing. "Now what's up with him?" They laughed behind his back, and Lactarius laughed along with them, but not in a cruel way, since sadness, he thought, suited his esteemed general, lending him more elegance than that baseless cheer, or that cheer based on dubious company, which had something vulgar about it. The legionaries, for their part, found this severe reserve more normal than the smiling fatuity of the previous days. Fulgentius himself felt that all was in order again, after a brief season of insanity. And sadness had the advantage of quenching the desire to think, leaving him free to contemplate the landscape.

JANUARY 25, 2017